Carry On
Up the Khyber

*The wickedly funny story that
starts where the film ends*

Norman Giller

Chameleon

For Alexander, Katharine, Charlotte and Jeremy
Carry on being grandchildren

First published in Great Britain in 1996 by
Chameleon Books
106 Great Russell Street
London WC1B 3LJ

CIP data for this title is available
from the British Library

ISBN 0 233 99030 5

Typeset by Falcon Oast Graphic Art

Printed in Great Britain by WBC, Bridgend

Author's Acknowledgements

This book could not have been written without the original foundation work of *Carry On* film creators Peter Rogers and Gerald Thomas. I have simply carried on where they left off, but I would not even have managed the first step without their marathon screen productions to inspire me. I am also indebted to the *Carry On* team of actors, who brought their characters to life on screen and turned the film series into a national institution. I acknowledge, too, the beautifully crafted screenplays of the writers, in particular Talbot Rothwell and Norman Hudis. On behalf of the Publishers, I thank the Rank Organisation for allowing us to step into the *Carry On* territory that has always been exclusive to the silver screen, and for their permission to use still photographs from the original film version of *Carry On Up the Khyber*.

My thanks also to VCI Chief Executive Steve Ayres for letting me off the leash, and to Tim Forrester, Tom Rosenthal and John Cleary at Chameleon Books for their encouragement; also to my House Editor Stephanie Goodwin, and to Richard Percy, who first had the brainwave to turn the *Carry On* films into books. Most of all, thanks to Eileenalanna, Lisa and Michael for being there.

The characters and events depicted on the following pages are entirely fictitious, and anybody who wishes to argue otherwise will be laughed out of court. *Carry On Laughing...*

Introduction

This book carries on where the film *Carry On Up the Khyber** left off. The story so far:

Sir Sidney Ruff-Diamond (Sidney James) is Her Majesty's Governor of the North West Frontier province of Kalabar. The Khyber Pass comes into his territory where invading tribesmen are always kicking up a stink.

The kilted Third Foot and Mouth Regiment, known to their enemies as 'Devils in Skirts' and to some of their friends as very nice boys, take on the dreaded Burpas, led by the sword-swirling giant Bunghit Din (Bernard Bresslaw). Private James Widdle (Charles Hawtrey) is caught with his pants on – under his kilt – and the Burpas are lured into thinking the 'Devils' have turned into wimps. But they give the invading Burpas a kick up the Khyber.

They relax in the intoxicating atmosphere of the out-of-bounds harem of the cunning Khasi of Kalabar (Kenneth Williams), who has so many wives that he cannot keep them all happy. The Third Foot and Mouth Regiment proceed to show them exactly what they have under their kilts. The Khasi is not aware of what is

*The classic comedy film *Carry On Up the Khyber* is available in the *Carry On* series on Cinema Club videos, distributed by VCI, price £4.99.

going on because he is too busy showing Lady Ruff-Diamond (Joan Sims) what a large scabbard he has. Sir Sidney, meantime, is deep in the valley of veils with the Khasi's First Wife (Wanda Ventham). Brother Belcher (Peter Butterworth) is fighting a losing battle trying to preach the word of the Lord to the Khasi and his followers, who finish up converting him.

This book takes the story on five years to the dawn of a new century. Sir Sidney Ruff-Diamond is still stuck in his boring rut as the Governor of Kalabar, his life made easier only by the fact that he has a staff of one hundred servants waiting on his every whim. The Third Foot and Mouth have been relieved by the Fourth Foot and Mouth under the direction of Captain Cardew Ffortescue-Ffortescue (Cardew Robinson) and Sergeant-Major Llandudno Thomas (who sounds very much like Windsor Davies).

Lady Ruff-Diamond has now become completely besotted by the cunning Khasi, and has joined his harem as a lay person. Sir Sidney is wondering how he can earn promotion to a more attractive post and win back his wife when Mudyard Tipling (Charles Hawtrey in a change of roles), the teller of tales and the world's worst poet although he doesn't know it, arrives with news of a plot being planned by the scheming Goondhi (Kenneth Connor). Can Sir Sidney get to the bottom of it before he, along with the British troops, are blown to the wind? Or will Ginga Don the fanwallah (Jon Pertwee, an old *Carry On* favourite) wave and save the day?

Now Curry On... sorry, I'll write that again, *Carry On reading...*

6

1

MAFEKING had been relieved, the creaking Queen Victoria was on the throne, the cunning Khasi of Kalabar was on the khasi, and the scheming Sir Sidney Ruff-Diamond was on the rampage. He had just got wind of some nasty goings-on up the Khyber Pass, and that was one place where only ill winds blew.

'What a ruddy curry on,' Sir Sidney said as he read a bottom-blowing report from secret agent Mudyard Tipling, who had managed to infiltrate the revolting Burpas in his undercover role as a teller of tales. 'This is going to cause a great stink back in London. The old Queen will be furious, and Her Majesty will be upset 'n' all.'

'If you can sort this out, you're a better man than I am Gunga Din,' said Mudyard, straightening his turban that had been loosened during his painfully slow retreat from up the Khyber on an elephant that would not use the trunk roads. 'They are replacing their gunpowder with curry powder ready for a mass attack on the British forces and ruling authorities like your good self.'

Sir Sidney's mind raced as he sat on the verandah of his palatial up-country residence where he was waited on hand and foot and eye, nose and mouth by a whirl of willing wallahs. He could envisage himself going down in history as the man who uncovered The Great

Curry Powder Plot (well, he would try to remember to give Mudyard a little of the credit... as little as possible). It was on a par with The Great Gunpowder Plot only potentially more explosive. Guy Fawkes, after all, was only going to blow up the Houses of Parliament, and there are plenty who would have considered that an exceedingly good idea. But this Curry Powder Plot was a threat to the British Empire and to Queen Victoria's imperialistic presence in India. If he could get to the bottom of the plot, it could, he thought, lead to a peerage (Earl Ruff-Diamond of the Khyber Pass) and release from the slow-death boredom of his job as Her Majesty's Governor of the North West Frontier province of Kalabar. It could also mean winning back his wife, Lady Ruff-Diamond, from the clutches of the cunning Khasi of Kalabar, who had enticed her into joining his harem as a lay person.

British Army Commander-in-Chief General Kitchener and his battle-weary cronies had their hands full with the Boer War in South Africa, where just the previous month Mafeking had been relieved. Sir Sidney knew he would have to deal with this crisis on his own to save India for Queen Victoria, who considered it the jewel in her crown. It would be down to him to make sure that the sun never set on her Empire. He would personally see to it that the map of the world would largely remain, like his gin, pink.

'What exactly do they hope to achieve with this curry powder plot?' asked Sir Sidney, snapping out of his day dream. 'And who's behind it?'

'Ah, just so,' said Mudyard, who really had a way

with words. 'You use the appropriate phrase, "behind it". The great plan is to blow off all the behinds of the British. The curry is a particularly strong vindaloo, and will have such an effect on the British soldiers that they will have no stomach for the fight.'

Mudyard looked at some scribblings on a blotchy notepad. 'I wrote a little poem about it on my way down from the Khyber Pass,' he said, 'if I may crave your indulgence...'

He cleared the three-day dust of the mountain passes from his throat, spat into the spittoon and read aloud:

'If you can keep your behind when all about you are
    losing theirs,
If you can have the runs, and having had them still be
    standing,
If you can digest a vindaloo, and having digested it leave
    the loo,
If you can curry favour, and having curried it then enjoy
    the curry flavour,
If you can have a red hot Indian, and having had one
    not drink the Ganges dry,
Yours is the Empire and everything that's in it,
    And, which is more, you'll be a Man, my son.'*

'If, if, bloody if,' said Sir Sidney. 'Sounds a bit iffy to me. If my Aunt Fanny had balls she'd be a man, my son. It's no good saying "if". Now is a time to be

*Author's note: I should be hung, drawn and sixteenthed for this parody of Rudyard Kipling's classic 'If' poem. If you have not read Kipling, I beseech you to do so, and enjoy the work of a master poet and teller of tales.

positive, and I am going to get to the bottom of this and kick a few backsides. So tell me, just who is the brains behind it? It's not that Musthafa Shyte, is it?'

Mudyard shook his turbaned head. 'There's a green-eyed yellow monster north of Katmandu,' he said. 'Well, he lives next door to a little brown man who wears large babies' napkins and walks around bare-foot. His name is Goondhi.'

'And this is the man who plans to bring down the British India Empire?' said Sir Sidney, scoffing. 'Don't make me laugh. You'll be telling me next that he plans to do it peacefully and without bloodshed.'

'Have you been peeping at my notes?' said an aggrieved Mudyard. 'That's it exactly. This is why he wants to use curry powder instead of gunpowder. Goondhi preaches passive resistance and non-violent confrontation as the way to rid India of the British.'

'But India *is* British,' roared Sir Sidney. 'We discovered it.'

'I had no idea that it was lost,' said Mudyard.

Sir Sidney ignored him. 'We're not having some bloody barefoot foreigner dressed in a baby's nappy telling us what to do,' he said. 'Where would they be without us? Just last night the Maharajah of Bagwash was telling me how much he owed the British.'

'Yes,' said Mudyard, 'I did hear that it was one hundred million rupees in back taxes for allowing him to farm his own land.'

'Yes, but we protect him from the Burpas and any other devilish dervishes who try to invade through the Khyber Pass.'

'Just so,' said Mudyard, 'but who protects them from the British?'

'Careful, Mudyard,' warned Sir Sidney, 'You are beginning to talk like one of them.'

Mudyard took his left hand off his hip.

'I think you're spending so much time in their company,' continued Sir Sidney, 'that you are becoming contaminated. Why, man, you're even wearing their clothes. You'll be baking poppadoms next.'

'You seem to forget that I am pretending to be one of them,' said Mudyard as his thick, toothbrush moustache bristled with indignation. 'My first loyalty remains to the old Queen.'

'General Kitchener will be pleased,' said Sir Sidney. 'We must crush this uprising before it picks up pace. God, if we were to lose India, the next thing you know those convicts down in Australia will be wanting to turn that land of ours into a Republic. Now then, this Goon chap...'

'Goondhi.'

'Whatever. How can we get to him? We've just got the 4th Foot and Mouth Regiment arrived from South Africa after the relief of Mafeking, thank God. They've relieved us of the 3rd Foot and Mouth who were the biggest bunch of idiots ever to disappear with a flash and a bang up the Khyber.'

'Begging your pardon, sir, but I doubts it very much. My boys is an even bigger bunch of hidiots.'

Sir Sidney looked up from his glass of gin into the ruddy face of Sergeant-Major Llandudno Thomas, known throughout the regiment as Doubting Thomas

11

because he doubted just about everything. He was a guest at the Governor's residence along with the Captain of the regiment, Cardew Ffortescue-Ffortescue, while being briefed as to their duties. They had arrived from the Boer War front just a week earlier, and already Sir Sidney had formed the opinion that they had each crossed a bridge too far and had a battle too many. Both were shot away.

The Captain and the Sergeant-Major joined Sir Sidney and Mudyard on the verandah where a team of charwallahs served them finest Indian tea in best English bone china cups, and they had a fanwallah each to protect them from the suffocating heat.

'Ah, Captain,' said Sir Sidney. 'You're just in time. Have you met Mudyard Tipling?'

'Tudyard Mippling?' said the Captain, who was spoonering long before Spooner introduced Spoonerism to the English language. 'Can't say I have. Not met any natives. Been on the lashed davatory ever since I got here.'

'Mudyard's not one of them,' said Sir Sidney.

Mudyard took his right hand off his hip.

'He's one of us.'

'Groodness gacious,' said Ffortescue-Ffortescue, so called because his mother had not wanted to drop her maiden name when marrying her cousin. 'He looks like one of them to me.'

Mudyard pulled in his lips and gave a deep-throated cough to underline his masculinity.

'He's a master of disguise,' explained Sir Sidney, 'and is our top agent out here.'

The Captain and the Sergeant-Major were impressed, as was Ginga Don the fanwallah, who was paid two rupees a day to report to the Khasi of Kalabar on anything he overheard.

'He's just brought news of a dastardly plot to blow off all British behinds with curry powder,' said Sir Sidney.

'Loo tate,' said the Captain. 'They've already got me.'

'I doubt if they could get me and my chaps, sir,' said the Sergeant-Major. 'We's have cast-iron stomachs after living on nothing but dried biscuits and snake entrails while under siege in Mafeking.'

'My goodness,' said Mudyard, 'you must have been relieved when you were relieved, if you follow me.'

'It was a relief, yes sir,' said the Sergeant-Major. 'We was tossing up as to which member of the Foot and Mouth regiment we would eat first. My name came out of the 'at, and I was ready to be eaten for my Queen and country. My only stipulation was that nobody should eat my private parts. A bit sensitive there, I is sir.'

'Quite,' said Sir Sidney. 'Now what we have to do is come up with a counter-plot against their ringleader, a little brown man with bare feet and wearing a baby's nappy.'

'A naby's bappy?' scoffed Ffortescue-Ffortescue. 'We'll just sheat the bit out of him.'

'No, it's going to need something much more subtle than that,' said Sir Sidney. 'This is a man who, by all accounts, practises and preaches non-violence.'

'Them's the kind of enemies I likes, sir,' said the Sergeant-Major. 'I doubts if we will have any trouble

13

kicking him out of India.'

'He claims this is his country and that it is the British who should be gently kicked out,' said Mudyard.

'I've never heard such nuff and stonsense,' said the Captain. 'This is Veen Quictoria's country, Bod Gless her. This bad and a counder isn't named Gandhi by any chance, is he?'

'No, it's Goondhi,' said Mudyard. 'But he believes in the same ideals and philosophies as Gandhi, who is working at the moment as a lawyer in South Africa. He keeps in close contact with his followers here in India.'

'Yes, he's been stirring it up in South Africa,' said the Captain. 'He's trying to tell the clacks and the boloureds that they should have equal wites as the rhites. I ask you. What is the corld woming to?'

'Too bloody true,' said Sir Sidney. 'Why everybody cannot just accept that the British way is the best way... is the *only* way... I'll never know.'

There were murmurs of assent, including a vigorous nodding of the head by Ginga Don the fanwallah, who also got two rupees every day from the chief wallah for agreeing with everything that Sir Sidney said and so keeping him in a good mood. 'It is a bloody disgusting shame, that it is Sahib sir,' said Ginga Don in a sing-song voice that could have been set to the music of the sitar. 'Goodness gracious, the British way is most surely the best. God Bless the old Queen. Rule Britannia.'

'Y'see,' said Sir Sidney, 'even the wallahs agree. Now if we were to react violently against Goondhi and his goons, we could lose the goodwill of the vast majority of Indians who obviously want British rule. We must

14

keep the support of the likes of this fanwallah here.'

Ginga Don the fanwallah smiled his broadest smile as he made a mental note to report to Goondhi about the Governor's reaction to his curry powder plot. He was being paid two rupees a day to keep Goondhi informed about anything said in the Governor's residence.

'Have you any ideas, gentlemen, how we can bring down Goondhi without resorting to violence?' asked Sir Sidney as he tipped his tea into the spittoon and filled his cup with gin.

'How about getting him involved in a scex sandal,' said the Captain. 'Are there any lase loodies around with whom we can tempt him?'

'I certainly hopes so,' said the Sergeant-Major, who had not set eyes on a woman, loose or tight, since leaving Blighty eighteen months ago.

'There are a few tasty goers in the Khasi of Kalabar's harem,' said Sir Sidney, talking from enjoyable experience. 'But it's easier to get into the Bank of England than into his harem. He has it guarded as if they were all his wives.'

'But they are, aren't they?' said the Captain.

'All except one,' said Sir Sidney with a mixture of shame and sadness. 'My wife is shacked up with him.'

'Your wife?' said Captain Incredulous.

Sir Sidney nodded. 'She found out that I was having a bit of a nibble on the side in the harem,' he said, 'and decided she couldn't beat them and so joined them.'

'Chough teese,' said Ffortescue-Ffortescue. 'This is a dit bifficult to say, but could your wife be used to tempt the little brown man in the naby's bappy?'

15

Sir Sidney considered commenting that he seemed to find *everything* a bit difficult to say. 'My wife would tempt any red-blooded man,' he said, 'but she's besotted by the Khasi. With the Great Curry Powder Plot about to engulf us, I must not let personal feelings get in the way of my duty to my Queen and country. First I must take care of Goondhi, and then I shall get even with the Khasi.'

Ginga Don the fanwaller sucked in this reference to Lady Ruff-Diamond. She was paying him two rupees a day to tell her everything the Governor said about her.

Mudyard, who had been busy writing a poem, looked up from his notepad. 'I must tell you, gentlemen, that you are wasting your time trying to tempt Goondhi with a girlie,' he said. 'He has been a contented partner in an arranged marriage since he was thirteen and has never been known to as much as look at another woman. I have written a little poem about the situation, if I may crave your indulgence...'

He cleared more of the dust of the mountain passes from his throat, spat into the spittoon and read aloud:

'There is an Indian man in a big hurry
To make gallons of red hot vindaloo curry.
    It will be fed to the Brits
    To blow their behinds to bits
And rocket them back to Surrey.'

The Governor, the Captain and the Sergeant-Major were speechless. Ginga Don the fanwallah was impressed. 'Goodness gracious,' he said, 'that is a most beautiful poem, oh great and glorious teller of tales. I will relate to my parents, grandparents, brothers, my sisters, my uncles, my aunts and all my friends that this is truly a poem of exceptional wisdom and wonder.'

He had agreed a fee of two rupees a day with Mudyard to help spread his poetry to try to make him as popular as his idol Rudyard Kipling.

'This is no time for poetry, this is time for action,' said Sir Sidney. 'Now what are we going to do to stop the plot of this clot.'

He was quietly pleased with his own stab at poetry. Kipling, eat your heart out.

'I doubts if you would want to hear the thoughts of an 'umble Sergeant-Major like what I am, sir,' said Thomas, 'but 'as you considered finding out where all this curry powder is being stored and having it blown up, sir?'

'What a wapital cheeze,' said Ffortescue-Ffortescue. 'We will send out pearch sarties first ting thomorrow.'

'Yes, that's a bright idea, Sergeant-Major,' said Sir Sidney. 'This way there will be no bloodshed, just a bit of curry scattering. But we need some really good military intelligence. Mudyard can't be everywhere at once.'

He looked around for inspiration and found himself gazing through his gin-sodden stare into the always grinning face of the fanwallah.

'Fanwallah,' he said, 'what's your name?'

'It is Ginga Don, oh mighty one,' said Ginga, dropping into a salaaming position expected of all servants when addressed by a superior. As just about

17

everybody was considered superior to Ginga, even though he had worked his way up to the esteemed position of fanwallah, he spent much of his life in a crouch. Little wonder that he had become prone to backache.

'How would you like to earn an extra two rupees a day on top of what I pay you?' said Sir Sidney, not realising that the two rupees went directly into the pocket of the chief wallah. He paid the team of wallahs under him by letting them eat as much as they liked of the food left over from the Governor's daily banquets.

'That would be most exceedingly kind of you, Lord and Master,' said Ginga Don, now heaping garlands of jasmine and roses on to the Governor. 'I am prepared to do anything you command to help you, your mightiness, and the great Queen Victoria, Empress of India, God Bless her. What is it that your worshipfulness requires of Ginga Don, the unworthy?'

'I want you to do a little spying for the Queen,' said Sir Sidney, knowing that the thought of working directly for Her Majesty would bring the best out of the little man lying prone in front of him.

'It would be the greatest honour of my entire existence,' said Ginga. 'The Queen's word is my command.'

'You are to work closely with Mudyard Tipling, and report back to me on anything you see or hear to do with the storing of curry powder,' said Sir Sidney. 'Pay particular attention to a fanatic called Goondhi. Do you know of this man?'

'Everybody in the entire universe is aware of

18

Goondhi,' said Ginga. 'There's a green-eyed yellow monster north of Katmandu. He lives next door.'

'What the devil is he doing in Nepal?' said Sir Sidney. 'Seems strange that a man seeking the independence of India should choose to live in a neighbouring country.'

'You misunderstand,' explained Mudyard. 'The green-eyed yellow monster north of Katmandu has moved to India and lives next door to Goondhi. He is his protector, and lets nobody near him without Goondhi's permission.'

'Grood gief,' said the Captain. 'What sort of monster is it?'

'Have you heard of the Abominable Snowman?' asked Mudyard.

'Not yet,' said the Captain.

'Well you soon will. The monster is related to him and is just as difficult to track down. Only a handful of people have clapped eyes on it.'

'What does it look like?' asked the Sergeant-Major.

'Abominable,' said Mudyard. 'In fact I've written a poem about...'

Sir Sidney got in quickly before Mudyard could bore him with another of his poems. 'That's settled then,' he said. 'Mudyard and Ginga Don are to give us a full report on the movements of Goondhi, the monster and the whereabouts of the curry powder before the plot thickens.'

Ginga Don nodded and grinned. The monster was paying him twenty rupees a day to report on everything that the British were planning.

Mudyard Tipling
A self portrait

THE OLD DELHICATESSEN

There once was a soldier in Old Delhi,

Who crawled around on his belly.

  He was extremely worried

  That he had been curried,

But it was his socks that were very smelly.

Mudyard Tipling
British India, 1900

20

2

THE cunning Khasi of Kalabar nodded knowingly as he received his two rupees worth of Ginga Don's listening service. He had long suspected that Mudyard Tipling was a British spy, mainly because he never seemed sure which way to wear his turban. He decided that he would one day order that his tongue be cut out to silence him; not because of his spying activities but because of his dreadful poems that were an assault to the ears and an insult to the intelligence. The Khasi had bought an honours degree in literature at Oxford University, and had a good ear and eye for poetry, its cadence and its scanning. Mudyard had a bad tongue for it, and it would have to come out. Omar Khayyam, Rudyard Kipling he was not. His rhyming days were numbered (or, the Khasi thought, should that be literalled?).

It was just a matter of timing. The Khasi did not want Mudyard muffled before he had uncovered exactly who was behind the Great Curry Powder Plot. It could not, he considered, be that little irritant Goondhi acting alone. Goondhi and his kind were an even bigger threat to him and his privileged lifestyle than the British imperialists. He wanted an equal society, with the rich sharing with the poor. What a nerve. The man was obviously quite insane.

The Khasi was rich beyond anybody's wildest dreams, his backside literally hanging with diamonds that were sewn into his silk pantaloons. Why should he

21

share this wealth with any man not intelligent enough to have inherited it? Goondhi was a well-educated man, but not well-educated enough to see that to make the status quo work the rich had to get richer so that they could throw out occasional crumbs to the poorer. It was as simple as that, but he was too blinded by his passion for equality to see it.

A man so extraordinarily dumb could not possibly be planning the Curry Powder Plot alone. How would he be able to get together the tons of curry powder needed for an explosive mission of this magnitude? No, there was somebody else's evil hand at work, and he would wait for Mudyard to find out who before literally silencing him. As for Goondhi, he would let history deal with him. There was no way in a million years that somebody preaching non-violence could possibly succeed in overthrowing something as mighty and victorious as Her Majesty's British Empire. Why, next they would be saying they could put a man on the moon.

The Khasi was following events as closely as a beggar counting his offerings. He did not mind his fellow Indians seeking independence from Britain, but he did not want somebody else ruling the country who would try to diminish the power of the Princes, the Maharajahs and the Khasis. He worked on the 'better the devil you know' principle, and the average Brit, he was delighted to find, was a simple, slow-thinking devil who he could easily outwit.

What interested him much more than the Curry Powder Plot was the news from Ginga Don that the foolish, fatuous, flatulent Governor wanted his wife back. 'Oh Great Allah, master of all we survey, I wish with all my heart and every organ in my body, particularly the organ that I use most of all, that you would rid me of this awful woman,' he said aloud in a peculiar nose-pinched nasal whine.

The Governor wanted her back? He could have her back, no questions asked. In fact the Khasi would throw in ten elephants, a herd of goats and his secret recipe for making the best korma in Kalabar if he would take her off his hands. But Lady Ruff-Diamond had made it clear that she was with the Khasi for life, and it was a life sentence that the Khasi could not rescind. He had stupidly made a vow of lasting love and obedience in a peak of passion during his first taste of her forbidden fruit. It was agreed as they lay together in their post-coital position sharing the dizzy delights of the smoke barrel that she should join his harem in an advisory capacity.

'I will be a special lay person and help organise your wives,' she had said in that cut-glass English accent of hers that was at first charming and now almost as irritating to his ears as Mudyard Tipling's poetry. Well, almost.

The Khasi wished ten thousand curses on the day he had given in to her advances, and kicked himself for making a vow that he could not break for fear that Allah would tear out his organs and feed them to the vultures. He had often suggested to her that she might be happier in her own environment back home in England, and that he would pay her fare – a single boat ticket – out of his own pantaloon pockets, but she would silence him with a stare that sent icicles dancing up and down his spine.

Since starting her lay person duties, she had virtually taken over the running of the palace and she had injected an atmosphere almost of revolt among his previously very well satisfied – in every sense – forty-seven wives. He had lately been subjected to a response he had never heard before Lady Ruff-Diamond's arrival: 'Not tonight, I have a headache.'

The Khasi had always taken the pick of his wives to suit any mood he might be in. There were the gentle ones, the passionate ones, the coy ones, the adventurous ones, the passive ones, the wild ones, the slender ones and the ones with big knockers. Now it all had to be on a strict rota, so that each of the wives was serviced in turn. 'It is only fair,' preached Her Ladyship. 'All your wives and I have our needs, and it is your duty to see to them.'

Away from the bedroom, there was an even bigger crisis brewing all because of that damned English woman's interference. Number One wife had acted as spokeswoman when a delegation came to see him. 'We want housekeeping,' she had said.

'Oooh, stop mucking about,' spluttered the Khasi. 'You do not even have a house to keep. You live in my palace and I pay for all the upkeep.'

'It is not good enough,' said Number One wife, who until being influenced by her snake-tongued adviser had never said anything more than 'more please'. She demanded that they each receive ten rupees a week plus a special clothes allowance, otherwise – and this shook the Khasi to the very core – there would be a ban on humping and grunting.

The Khasi had decided to call their bluff, and said, 'Fair enough. No humping and grunting it is.'

In the past, a mutiny such as this would have been quickly ended by one of the wives – the ugliest one – having her head chopped off in front of the rest of them as a salutary lesson. The Khasi had in fact had one wife executed because she had had the nerve to question his performance in bed – him, the great stud of Kalabar.

But Her Ladyship had warned that any act of retribution against the wives would result in her ordering her husband to have him arrested and charged under British law which, as that true teller of tales, Charles Dickens, had revealed to the world, was an ass.

It was now a week since the stand-off had started, and he was beginning to suffer terrible withdrawal symptoms, withdrawal being the operative word. What he could not understand is how his wives, all forty-seven of them, could manage to look so contented. Perhaps it was something to do with the smiles on the faces of the harem guards, or could it be that the fallen Brother Belcher had resurfaced?

The Khasi had warned him off a year ago after finding him being converted by his wives. Brother Belcher had come from England to spread the gospel, but had finished up being spread on the floor of the harem. The Khasi had driven him away by threatening to convert him to the Jewish faith with an instant circumcision.

First, the Khasi decided, it would be off with

Mudyard Tipling's tongue. Then it would be off with the testicles of his guards if he found any had not been properly eunuched, and then Brother Belcher would be converted to the Sisterhood. The humping and grunting ban was quite definitely affecting his mood. 'No wonder I've got the right hump,' he grunted to himself. 'I must rid myself of that woman. But how?' Then, praise be to Allah, it came to him. He would see to it that she got wind of the Great Curry Powder plot.

Lady Ruff-Diamond nodded knowingly as she received her two rupees worth of Ginga Don's listening service. It did not concern her in the slightest that Sir Sidney was desperate to have her back. He had been the one who first cheated on her, and had broken the marriage vows. Now she had found a world that was a paradise far away from the narrow restrictions, snobbery and self-righteous claptrap of the life she had left behind. She had a diamond as big as a boulder for every finger, and she could hardly hold up her head because of the weight of the jewelled necklaces draped around her. 'Goodness, Khasi-wasi,' she had said, 'many more and you could break my neck.' He had since insisted on giving her a new necklace every single day.

There was the added bonus of wonderful soul-reaching, earth-moving, knee-trembling humpty rumpty, as Sir Sidney called it. It was only on every forty-eighth day, but that was a big improvement on what she got from her husband. And what he had to give her was, frankly, not a lot.

From the moment she became the official adviser to

the harem she saw it as her duty to improve the lot of those poor put-upon, downtrodden wives. The pitiable dears were treated as nothing better than doormats and the occasional bed mattress. Nobody had ever introduced them to the great art of nagging. Lady Ruff-Diamond had been taught by a true artist. Her mother nagged her father into an early grave, and had since gone through two more husbands with a tongue that could have sliced through rhino skin.

Each day Her Ladyship, as she was known throughout the palace, gave lessons in how to nag the Khasi into giving them what they wanted. She taught them foot-stamping, door-slamming, tongue-lashing, mock crying, sullen silences, the cold-stare/hands-on-hips challenging position and, her mother's particular favourite, how to cock a deaf 'un. 'Give him a deaf ear but never a blind eye,' Mother had advised the best-forgotten day she married Sir Sidney Ruff-Diamond while Daddy held a blunderbuss to his back. She had just a few weeks earlier been able to give Sir Sidney the good news that he was not sterile, but the baby had been lost after a five month pregnancy and then her ambitious husband had become too involved in his career with the diplomatic corps to give any more attention to starting a family.

Their initial excitement in landing a governorship at Kalabar had given way to disappointment and then despair when they realised how barren and remote it was, and far too close to the warmongering factions at the Khyber Pass for comfort. The revolting Burpas, fired up by their crazed leader Bunghit Din, made continual raids on the surrounding villages and disturbed Her

Ladyship's beauty sleep. And she needed lots of it.

She was surrounded by hand maidens, foot maidens and servants for every function of her body, but this added to rather than alleviated her boredom. In her lowest moment she had written home to her mother, 'Oh to be in England now that April's here. I know you told me, Mummy, that I should always do my duty to my husband, my Queen and my country, but it is awfully hard lying on my back and thinking of England when my husband has his mind on other matters and not on our mattress. I have discovered that he is having his humpty rumpty at the harem of the local Khasi. I shall follow the advice that you gave me when you found out that Daddy was having a little on the side. I am going to do exactly what you did: tie his testicles to the bed post when he is fast asleep and then shout "Fire".'

Then, before she could put her dramatic plan into action, the Khasi of Kalabar had come into her life and had awakened passions and feelings that she did not even realise she possessed. She did not know what it was about him, but there was an attraction like a magnetic force. Perhaps it was his well-hung scimitar, the way his nostrils flared when he laughed, the tilt of his turban, the bulge in his jodhpurs where he kept his curved dagger, or perhaps, just perhaps, it was the diamonds, rubies and opals that hung from him like presents on a Christmas tree.

She had made just two major *faux pas* since taking over the running of the palace. She had shooshed the cooks out of the kitchen one day and gave everybody at the palace a special treat: good old British roast beef with Yorkshire pudding and roast potatoes. 'Are you trying to drive everybody mad?' shouted the Khasi, while all around him wives were weeping and sobbing.

'British beef won't make you mad,' said Her Ladyship. 'That's just a silly old wives tale.'

'*Any* beef will make us mad,' said the Khasi. 'You will bring the curse of Allah down on this palace a thousandfold and all who dwell in here. Don't you realise that in India the cow is sacred and is to be worshipped and revered, and certainly not eaten. To Hindus, the cow is next to God.'

To make amends, the next day she cooked a huge, sumptuous leg of pork, with great dollops of apple sauce and lightly roasted potatoes. More weeping and sobbing, and another lecture from a Khasi who was quite beside himself. 'You silly, silly Ladyship,' he said. 'Don't you understand that pork, anything to do with a pig, is offensive and forbidden to Muslims.'

'Hindus, Muslims, Sikhs,' thought Her Ladyship. 'It's all far too confusing and complicated. Next, they'll be telling me that I cannot touch the Untouchables.'

She kept out of the kitchen from then on, and just concentrated on getting the wives as well organised and disciplined as the voluntary service she had run at home in Cheltenham.

Her Ladyship introduced them to the great British tradition of knitting. In their first month, all knitting one, purling one – and occasionally dropping one – they completed what was supposed to have been a scarf but which was finally presented to the Khasi as a handkerchief. He was not as grateful as he might have been, complaining that the wool made his nose itch.

The wives were so thrilled to have been taught the knitty gritty of knitting that they clubbed together and gave Her Ladyship a signed copy of the Karma Sutra.

As the industrious Ginga Don knelt fanning her, she weighed up what Sir Sidney had and what the Khasi could give her. There was Sir Sidney's two hundred and fifty pounds a year salary, the free train, tram and omnibus travel and free horse stabling, the fifty pounds a year clothes and entertainment allowance, his five-bedroomed house in an acre of land in Cheltenham and his stiff upper lip. The Khasi was, conservatively, worth a hundred million pounds, had an eighty-roomed palace set in two hundred acres of beautifully landscaped gardens, enough jewels to sink a battleship, a staff of five hundred servants, a rumoured buried treasure, and, oh yes, he was continually stiff in a more appropriate place than his upper lip.

After careful consideration and taking everything into account, Her Ladyship came down on the side of the Khasi. She admitted that it had been quite a stiff choice.

She settled back deeper into the bejewelled cushions, smoothed out her silk sari, and wished that her forty-eighth night would hurry forward. But, of course, first the Khasi had to agree to pay housekeeping. Until then his wives would follow the most torturous of all her mother's negotiating positions: the crossed legs.

Ginga Don delivered his news and gossip like a postman would deliver letters or a milkman bottles of milk. His next call was on Goondhi, who nodded knowingly as

30

he received his two rupees worth of Ginga Don's listening service. It was no surprise to Goondhi that Mudyard Tipling was a British spy. He had realised it the first time he heard him reciting one of his poems. Anybody that illiterate could not possibly have been a true teller of tales.

Goondhi had listened to the best tellers of tales in the whole of India, and it was from them that he learned of the horrors perpetrated on the citizens of his country by soldiers of the Queen. The great Indian Rebellion of 1857 had been caused by Indian soldiers mutinying after they had been commanded by their British superiors to use bullet cartridges that had been greased with the fat of cows and pigs*.

This was abhorrent to their religious beliefs, and they turned their guns on their British masters. Thousands of them had been put to the sword and shot after they had first killed many British officers and their families in a bloody uprising. Clumsy and contemptuous attempts had been made to force Christianity on them, and this had led to a ground swell of opinion that it was time to end the era of the British Raj. Goondhi was determined to feed on the widespread view that the British had bled India dry of enough of its treasures and wealth. They now wanted them out, peaceably if possible.

Goondhi had attended meetings where gunpowder was continually put forward as the substance that should be used to get the British out. He and an anonymous sponsor had suggested the alternative and fairly unusual idea of using curry powder instead. At first everybody had

*Author's note: This is not the usual *Carry On* fiction. This is fact.

31

laughed until they realised that he and the extremely influential man supporting him were deadly serious. So the Great Curry Powder Plot was born.

It did not unduly worry Goondhi that the British had found out about the plot because he was sufficiently confident that they could get the plan to work even if they managed to track down some of the powder. There were sufficient supplies hidden around the country to ensure that there would be enough to cause a mass explosion at British army camps and government establishments across the country.

'The British can mock my baby's napkin, which is in fact a simple sheet, all they wish,' said Goondhi to the ever-smiling Ginga Don. 'There is an old British saying that I learned at Cambridge University, "He who laughs last laughs longest". I and all my fellow Indians are going to have a very, very long laugh indeed.'

Ginga Don laughed and laughed, mainly because all the time the cross-legged Goondhi had been talking to him he did not realise that he had forgotten to put on his napkin. Goondhi was so preoccupied with his plot that he had become as absent-minded as an elephant with amnesia.

Ginga Don next went to the neighbouring home occupied by the green-eyed yellow monster, who nodded knowingly as he received his twenty rupees worth of Ginga Don's listening service. Ginga had no idea who was behind the monster's mask, and he did not particularly care while he was prepared to shell out so much dosh a day for all that the enterprising fanwallah could report on the fascinating world around him.

It was Ginga Don who had first spread the story that this was the green-eyed yellow monster from north of Katmandu in neighbouring Nepal. He had been handsomely paid fifty rupees for his work, and the tale had spread like wildfire, even to the extent of the British agent Mudyard hearing it while spying on the Burpas at the Khyber Pass, and, what is more, believing it.

The monster, who deliberately terrorised the local community to scare unwanted people away and stop any snoopers coming near Goondhi, digested everything that Ginga Don told him about the spy Mudyard, the fact that Sir Sidney knew all about the Curry Powder Plot and all his idle gossip about the Khasi and Lady Ruff-Diamond.

'You are a very good listener, Ginga Don,' the monster said, his voice deep and distorted behind the huge mask that covered his face and came down over his chest like a huge dragon's head. In the corner of the room was the rest of his realistic costume. 'Just never forget that only you know and Goondhi knows that there is a man behind this mask. If ever it were to become public knowledge, just bear in mind that it is your ears that I will tear off first. Do I make myself clear?'

Ginga Don was waving his fan furiously in front of his own face. 'You make yourself very clear oh great monster,' he said. 'My lips are as sealed as the door to the Black Hole of Calcutta.'

This was one secret that Ginga Don, the great messenger, would never pass on. He liked his ears too much. How could he do his work without them?

33

Mudyard Tipling
A self portrait

HELL IN THE HAREM

The Governor wants his wife back,
And the Khasi would like her to go,
But Her Ladyship refuses to pack,
Because she likes the harem so.
She acts as if she's the Khasi's wife,
And nags him something rotten,
She's made a misery of his life,
And happiness has been forgotten.

Mudyard Tipling
British India, 1900

34

3

IT was kit inspection time on the parade ground of Her Majesty's Fort Phucka that had been taken over and reinforced by the British in 1881 following the Second Afghan War. Situated within sight of the Khyber Pass, it was from here that British troops went out on patrols to guard the Pass and protect Queen Victoria's India from the threat of invasion. The remnants of the 4th Foot and Mouth Regiment were still adjusting to the different climes and times of India following their tour of duty in South Africa where they had just about survived the Siege of Mafeking.

Most, or indeed all, of the regiment's history had been about taking part rather than winning. The majority of the original members of the first Foot and Mouth were from Highland farming stock, and they had got their name when tackling and eradicating an outbreak of foot and mouth disease that threatened north of Scotland herds in the 1840s. The regiment had since been strengthened (said the English) or diluted (said the Scots) by an influx of English mercenaries interested only in earning the Queen's shilling.

They were appalled, petrified even, at the prospect of getting caught up in any action that might involve a) being shot at; b) speared; c) blown up; or, d to z) being put into danger of any nature whatsoever.

There were, of course, exceptions. Sergeant-Major Llandudno Thomas thrived on meeting the enemy head on and liked to lead from the front. Trouble was he usually found that when looking back over his shoulder only a handful of stouthearts had followed his lead. But he was confident that on this Indian assignment they would rise to the occasion and write an illustrious page in the regiment's history, particularly when his soldiers learned they were to face an enemy that did not believe in violence.

True Scottish traditions were maintained in the regiment in that they were always led on parade and into battle by bagpipers, and the soldiers all wore kilts. They had become widely known as the 'Devils in Skirts', a nickname that had been well hung on them by the many women who had been fascinated to find out what they wore beneath the kilts. It was at times like this that they did manage to rise to the occasion in quite spectacular fashion.

The parade ground kit inspection of the 4th Foot and Mouth Regiment was unique in military history. It followed a ritual that had its roots in an event in India when a soldier in the 3rd Regiment had been captured by the Burpas. During a full body search he was found to be wearing knee-length pants under his kilt. This led to the regiment becoming a laughing stock among the revolting Burpas, who had been told they were real men's men. From then on the order went out that no Foot and Mouth soldier should ever be caught with his pants up.

With Captain Ffortescue-Ffortescue looking on from a raised dais in the centre of the Fort Phucka parade ground, Sergeant-Major Thomas roared the rather unusual command: 'Present charms!'

In one swirling movement, all the soldiers held up their kilts to show that they were properly, some might say improperly, dressed. The Sergeant-Major rapidly inspected each member with a well-practised turn of his head, his narrowed eyes beetling away from beneath the rim of his snow-white pith helmet.

He was satisfied that everybody had complied to the order, and that all weapons had been presented and exposed. In India's suffocating heat, much more humid and energy-draining than the dry heat of the South African veldt, they were relieved not to have to wear anything under the kilts. If it had not been for protocol, they would willingly have not worn their kilts or heavy, heat-attracting red tunics, either.

'Right, boyhos, attention!' barked the Sergeant-Major. 'Captain Ffortescue-Ffortescue will now haddress you on a matter of the hutmost himportance.'

'At chease aps,' said the Captain, who liked to adopt a casual, friendly demeanour, much to the undisguised disgust and despair of the strictly-by-the-book Sergeant-Major. 'I have today been biven the grief for our first major assignment here in British India. A punning clot has been uncovered to mestroy the dorale of the British army and government officials serving in Mer Hajesty's Indian Empire. We have been trusted with the jifficult dob of dracking town the cerpetrators of this prime.'

He looked proudly out at his regiment that had fought, or rather been besieged, with such dignity in South Africa. 'You will be pleased to learn,' he announced, 'that following our experiences in the Boer War, this is going to be a ciece of pake. Our enemy do not believe in garrying cuns and, so as not to antagonise them, we too will day lown our arms. When going out on patrols, you will leave your buns gehind.'

In the front rank of the parade Private Jock McKnacker and Private Harry Arden exchanged side-on glances. 'What is this mad mon going on aboot?' said McKnacker, moving his mouth like that of a ventriloquist working a dummy.

'Search me,' replied Arden, with a similar letterbox shape to his mouth and in an accent that instantly identified him as a Brummie. 'I can never understand a word he's saying, but I do know it sounds dangerous. I think a bit of fainting is called for.'

He immediately pitched forward on to the sandy parade ground, dropping his Enfield rifle at his side. McKnacker bent to pick him up.

'Leave him be,' yelled the Sergeant-Major, loud enough to be heard right up the Khyber Pass. 'If you're not hup within twenty seconds Private Harden you will be whitewashing this parade ground from now until midnight.'

Arden considered continuing his act, but thought better of it when he heard the Sergeant-Major's heavy tread approaching. Thomas reached him as he got to his feet. His face was now so close to Arden's that he could smell the garlic from last night's mess of a meal that had been prepared by the chefwallahs who managed to make everything they cooked taste, well, Indian. How he could do with some of his mum's dumpling stew, soaked in beef gravy and with lashings of mashed potatoes and juicy carrots.

'What d'you think you're up to, eh Harden?' he said through gritted teeth. 'I 'ad enough of you at Mafeking always asking to be relieved. Now don't try to come your clever tricks 'ere, boyho, 'cos I've got my heye on you and will make you pay for hany little sign or even so much has an 'int of hinsubordination.'

'Sorry, Sergeant-Major,' Arden said. 'I went all sort of faint and weak at the knees. It's this terrible heat. I can't stand it.'

'You *will* stand it,' said the Sergeant-Major. 'And I'll tell you why you'll stand it – because I says so. The 'eat is the same for all of hus. You don't find anybody helse falling about faint...'

The words were not completely out of his mouth when there was a crashing sound behind him. The Sergeant-Major turned to find Captain Ffortescue-Ffortescue lying face first in front of the dais. 'Right, you McKnacker and Arden,' he commanded, 'help the Captain back to his quarters, find him a shady place to lie and then come back 'ere to the parade ground double quick and listen to your horders.'

'Srightfully forry,' the giddy Captain mumbled as the two privates hauled him up off the floor, blood gushing from a deep gash on his nose. 'The gun sot to me.'

'Och, dinya worry aboot it, Captain,' said McKnacker as he helped Arden half carry him back across the parade ground to his quarters. 'It's hot enough tae burn the bum off an Angus bull.'

Sergeant-Major Thomas took over where the Captain left off. 'What the Captain was saying is that a secret plot 'as been uncovered to blow off our British behinds with curry powder,' he said.

There was a spontaneous outbreak of muttering.

'Q-u-i-e-t in the ranks,' the Sergeant-Major screamed. 'How dares you mutter when I is talking.'

He glared down at the massed ranks, bubbles of perspiration forming what looked like a row of pearls along his forehead immediately under the rim of his pith helmet. The merciless sun was beating down through the first cloud formation he had seen since arriving in India on a troopship from Cape Town.

'Now listen very closely, boyhos,' he said as chummily as he could manage. 'Our henemies knows that an Army marches on its stomach, and they has come hup with this plot to hempty our stomachs in a savage way that will leave us weak and defenceless. What we has decided to do is send out special search parties to find the curry powder what they is going to use.'

McKnacker and Arden had returned to their front-row positions. 'Permission to speak, sir,' Arden said, raising an arm.

'This 'ad better be himportant, Private Harden,' growled the Sergeant-Major. 'Not one of your usual stupid bloody questions.'

'What, sir,' said Arden with as straight a face as he could muster, 'does curry powder look like?'

'What a stupid bloody question,' said the Sergeant-Major. 'Hanybody knows that. It's sort of, uh, powdery. Lots of little grains.'

'What colour is it?' said Arden, enjoying himself.

The Sergeant-Major was struggling. He had never set eyes on curry powder in his life.

'Well, it's a sort of, uh, whitish, greyish, brownie colour,' he said. 'You'll soon know it when you sees it because number one, there'll be lots and lots of it, and, number two, you'll be able to smell that it's curry a mile away.'

The smell of curry drifted across the parade ground from the cook house where the chefwallahs were preparing that evening's meal. The Sergeant-Major twitched his nose, and his twirled military moustache moved up and down like the wings of a small bird.

'Take a niff of that,' he said. 'That's the curry we is looking for.'

'Shouldnae we be arresting the chefwallahs then?' said McKnacker, levelling his Enfield towards the cook house.

'No, you hidiot,' said the Sergeant-Major. 'They is on our side.'

'How do we know that?' asked Arden.

'Because they cooks for us every night.'

'Aye, and we're all being sicker than wee stray dogs in Sauchiehall Street every flippin' morning,' moaned McKnacker.

'It's whole mountains of curry we is looking for,' said the Sergeant-Major. 'Great stacks of the stuff. They couldn't hide that much in the cook house, but we'll hinterrogate them just in case. Meanwhile, I wants the first patrol, minus guns and not displaying weapons of any kind...'

'Does that mean we should put our underpants on?' Arden whispered out of the side of his mouth.

'...to go out now and search up the Khyber Pass.

41

That's all you bhoyos in the front rank.'

Arden raised an arm, and felt like raising two in surrender. 'Permission to speak, sir.'

'Yes, Arden. What is it this time?'

'Isn't the Khyber Pass where the revolting Burpas are based?'

'They is right on the other side of the Pass where the 3rd Foot and Mouth drove them during their tour of duty,' said the Sergeant-Major. 'We 'as only got to search this side of the Pass what his in British Hindia. We won't be going hanywhere near the Burpas.'

'I still think it would be wise to take our guns,' said Arden.

'What you thinks and what you does in the Queen's Army, boyho, is two different things,' said the Sergeant-Major. 'Our horders is no weapons, and so no weapons it is. Hunderstood, boyho?'

'Understood, sir,' said Arden.

'Och, nobody's going tae take my dirk off me,' McKnacker said quietly. His dagger had been his second most treasured weapon ever since his grandfather had sold it to him on his deathbed. He shifted it deep down out of sight inside his right sock.

The Sergeant-Major was just about to bark out more orders when the sky suddenly turned black as if somebody had thrown a huge blanket above the parade ground.

Every head on the parade ground looked up. 'What the bloody 'ell is going on?' said the Sergeant-Major.

'Who turned the gaslamp off?' said Arden.

'Och,' said wee Jock McKnacker, 'it's a broad licht

42

moonlicht nicht tonicht.'

Ginga Don, who had just arrived at the fort to carry out fanning duties at a banquet in the officer's mess, pointed to the jet-black clouds scudding overhead. 'The monsoon, king soldier, sir, is about to start,' he said, and even as he spoke heavy single drops of steaming warm rain began to fall as if from a giant dripping tap in the sky.

'It's only a few spots of rain,' said the Sergeant-Major, a veteran of many a rainstorm in the Welsh valleys. 'All right first patrol, guns down and off you go. Report back here four hours from now.'

'A thousand and one pardons, oh master,' said Ginga Don, salaaming in front of the Sergeant-Major. 'I would cut my heart out if I did not give you the fearful warning that this is something much more than just a few spots of rain.'

The twelve-strong patrol, with McKnacker and Arden reluctantly at the front, looked at the Sergeant-Major with pleading eyes, like dogs not wanting to go into the pound.

The Sergeant-Major held out the palms of his hands and felt the occasional heavy splash of rain. 'I doubts if this is anything more than just a passing shower,' he said. 'If you'd grown up in the valleys like what I did you would have known what real rain is like.'

'Permission to speak, sir,' said Arden.

'What is it, Harden? Do you want to be relieved again?'

'I was just wondering, sir, if it might be a good idea to take our waterproof capes.'

43

'What sort of a useless wimp are you, Arden?' said the Sergeant-Major. 'Frightened of a little drop of water is we? Hi've stood in the Valleys hunprotected when we've 'ad as much as three hinches of rain in just one 'our. Never did me hany 'arm.'

'Except it's shrunk his brain,' Arden said in a whispered aside to McKnacker.

'A thousand thousand pardons, sir,' said the still salaaming Ginga Don, 'but in the monsoon season we have as much rain as that in a minute.'

Sergeant-Major Thomas stepped purposefully down off the dais and stood in front of the unarmed first patrol. 'Come on, boyhos,' he said, always keen to show that he was willing to do whatever he asked of his men, 'I'll lead the way. You follow. It'll do us all good to get wet. Much better than being grilled all day by this bloody sun.'

He looked back over his shoulder and shouted across the parade ground. 'The rest of you,' he ordered, 'form patrols of twelve and be prepared to go out in turn the moment we gets back from the Khyber Pass. And remember, boyhos, no weapons. This is new, non-violent warfare.'

Thomas had led the patrol on a quick march a mile from the fort when the monsoon broke. Suddenly what seemed like a huge ferris wheel of water came rolling towards them. It did not appear to come from out of the sky but horizontally along the ground, high and wide and revolving as if turned by an unseen handle. It was being driven along by a wild wind that had whipped up from nowhere. Within seconds the

44

Sergeant-Major and everybody in the patrol was soaked through, and they clung on to each other to save themselves from being blown off their feet.

'We 'as one of two options,' the Sergeant-Major shouted above the roar of the torrent of water. 'We can either try to get back to the fort a mile that way,' he said, nodding his head from where they had come from, 'or we can look for shelter in the Khyber Pass three quarters of a mile that way.' He pointed ahead of them at the range of Safed Koh mountains through which the Khyber Pass had been carved centuries before.

Even three quarters of a mile seemed like a marathon in these conditions, but they decided to head for the Pass. Their decision was made for them by the fact that they found it impossible to walk into the whipping wind that was now driving at them from the direction of the fort. With it at their backs, they were pushed along as if by rough, invisible hands. The water was crashing off the ground and hitting them in the backs of their legs. Their red tunics were soaked black, their kilts were as sodden as seaweed on an ocean bed, and the privates were very wet indeed. They were half running and half stumbling along rocky terrain that was scuffing their boots and ripping holes in their socks. The black sky was being spectacularly lit by flashes of zig-zagging lightning, and the rain had changed from a revolving wheel into a solid wall.

Arden wanted to ask the Sergeant-Major if this made him homesick for the Valleys, but he could not get a single word out. To open the mouth would have meant taking the risk of drowning.

After what seemed like an hour they finally reached the opening to the Khyber Pass, deliberately narrowed with boulders and rocks by previous British Army regiments to make it harder for invading forces to get through.

With the Sergeant-Major leading the way, they battled single file into the Pass and looked for any cover or makeshift shelter as the rain continued to batter down on them, across them and through them. McKnacker was first to spot a large cave-like entrance off to the right, and as he pointed it out the thoroughly saturated Sergeant-Major indicated for the rest of the patrol to follow him.

They had just tumbled into the welcome dryness of what was clearly a man-made cave when behind them they heard the unmistakeable clicking sounds of a dozen rifles being cocked.

Sergeant-Major Thomas and his stunned patrolmen looked round as if their heads were being jerked by the same piece of wire. Staring menacingly back at them from behind raised rifles were a brigade of Burpas, sworn enemies of the Indians in general and of the British in particular.

Their leader, a huge man with a high turban that made his six foot five inch frame look much taller, grinned at them through broken, discoloured teeth. 'It is with a thousand thousand greetings that I welcome you to our humble little home,' he said with a deep bow and an even deeper voice that came up from his boots and boomed around the cave roof. 'It is most thoughtful of you to let us have the chance to see what the Devils

46

in Skirts are wearing under their skirts this year.'

Bunghit Din, the Burpas leader, roared with laughter, and then shot a hole clean through the top of Private Arden's waterlogged pith helmet.

Private Arden fainted, and this time he was not acting.

The Khyber Pass, strategically the most important point on the North West Frontier, is thirty-three miles long, ranging in width from three miles to just fifteen feet and reaching an elevation of 3,500 feet. For centuries the Pass had been a well-beaten path for a procession of invaders into India, with the Persians, the Moghuls, the Russians and the Afghans all taking turns to use the route to make uninvited visits. It had now become the prison of Sergeant-Major Thomas and his patrol, who were tied hand, foot and testicle in the cave into which they had wandered to try to avoid the monsoon. They were truly stuck up the Khyber.

Bunghit Din had fiendishly ordered that the rope tying them all together should be attached not only to their feet and hands but also to the private parts of the privates (and the Sergeant-Major), so that any sudden movement by one of the sodden soldiers would be immediately signalled by one or more of the others.

'What we needs, boyhos, is a clever plan to get ourselves out of this,' whispered the Sergeant-Major while Bunghit Din and his men were locked in an animated conference at the far end of the cave.

'We could try bargaining with them,' said Arden, his previous existence as a Birmingham town centre market stall holder coming to the surface. 'They're famous for their bartering in these parts.'

'Oh yes, boyho,' mocked the Sergeant-Major. 'And what do we offer them? Two pounds of potatoes for the price of one?'

'I thought we could offer them the whereabouts of the Khasi of Kalabar's treasure in return for our freedom,' said Arden.

'That's a good idea,' said the Sergeant-Major. 'Where is it exactly?'

Arden shrugged. 'I haven't got a clue.'

The Sergeant-Major was so exasperated that he kicked out at Arden, and the cave was suddenly alive with the yells and groans of twelve voices in an unheavenly chorus sounding even above the still-raging monsoon.

This brought Bunghit Din and his tribesmen scurrying over. 'Be quiet you infidels,' shouted the rebel leader. 'You are making enough noise to wake the mighty monster who will, I plead with you Allah, be washed away by the great rains.'

He drew a huge curved sword from the thick rope belt around his waist. 'We are at this moment deciding your fate,' he said. 'We want to know why you have dared come into our territory without arms. What cunning trap are you preparing to spring? You know that the Burpas have a proud tradition never to kill unarmed opponents, otherwise by now I would have personally cut off all your heads...'

He swished inches above their heads with his swirling sword.

'...after first, of course, slicing off what little you have beneath your skirts.'

48

The sword was now swishing just inches from the privates. Every member of the 4th Foot and Mouth patrol showed astonishing discipline as they stayed deadly still, knowing that the pain brought on by sudden movement was something that should, if at all possible, not be experienced again.

'We have come unharmed so that we can parley peace,' the Sergeant-Major ad-libbed. 'It his the horders of the Government of Her Majesty Queen Victoria, Hempress of all of Hindia...'

Bunghit Din stood stiffly to attention out of respect for a despised yet revered enemy.

'...that we should try to make peace with the Burpas. We 'as our 'ands full with those crafty Hindians what is trying to blow off our behinds with curry powder.'

'Ah, this I have heard,' said Bunghit Din. 'The great teller of tales, Mudyard Tipling, was made aware of it on his last visit here to the Khyber Pass. We, the revolting Burpas, do not hold with such tactics. War should be fought as war, not as child's play. Without war how do we exist? It is all that we know.'

Bunghit Din was now striding around the cave talking to his feet and waving his sword in a mixture of anger and irritation. 'How dare some pussy-footed, cowardly Indians try to make things work peaceably,' he said aloud to himself. 'What is this world coming to when people stop trying to kill each other? Civilised living will be the beginning of the end for us all. What were we put on earth for if it was not to kill, plunder, pillage and rape? What else is there left?'

He turned and faced the Sergeant-Major. 'I respect

you and your brave men for coming here unarmed,' he said. 'It is the act of courageous, if foolish, warriors. But I spurn Her Majesty Queen Victoria's offers of peace. We are violently opposed to any non-violent, non-aggression pact, and I am prepared to let you return to Fort Phucka to report the words of I, Bunghit Din. Just thank your gods a thousand thousand times that you came into my domain unarmed otherwise I would now be talking to dead men.'

It was just at this moment that the dirk buried in McKnacker's right sock worked its way loose through the hole made during the mad scramble across the rocky terrain. It fell on to the rock floor with a tinging sound that alerted the eyes and ears of the Burpas leader.

He looked down at the nine inch dagger lying at his feet, and his face turned a shade of purple.

'You have deceived me, you evil sons of Satan,' he roared. 'Now I sentence you all to instant death.'

He lifted his sword above his head ready to bring it down on Sergeant-Major Thomas, who instinctively shied away and with his sudden movement there were twelve voices raised in unison sounding not unlike the Welsh choir to which he had once belonged, although he could not remember so many sopranos. Then there was a contrasting deep-throated roar and a sudden spurt of flame from the direction of the cave entrance.

The Burpa tribesmen, with a terrified Bunghit Din bringing up the rear, raced to an exit at the far end of the cave as the green-eyed yellow monster from north of Katmandu made a dramatic entrance, spitting fire and whirling around as if dancing on hot coals. Bunghit

50

Din's behind was scorched as he scrambled out of the cave with his pantaloons on fire.

McKnacker picked up the dirk and quickly started cutting through the rope binding them painfully together.

'If we gets back to the fort alive, boyho, you is on a charge,' growled the Sergeant-Major. 'You was under strict orders, no weapons.'

He now switched his thoughts to the rather more pressing predicament of how to handle a man-burning monster. The thirteen members of the Foot and Mouth patrol stood with their backs to the cave wall, feeling as if they were about to be grilled ready for a final supper.

But then, as quickly as he had appeared, the monster turned on its heels and trotted out of the cave. Moments later Ginga Don salaamed his way into the cave. 'A thousand thousand pardons for interrupting you oh great and wonderful warriors of Her Majesty Queen Victoria, Empress of India, God Bless her,' he said. 'I was just worried that you might have got lost in the monsoon. Come, the rains have eased. Follow me and I will show you a short cut back to Fort Phucka, oh mighty ones.'

So it was that the bedraggled patrol, no nearer getting to the bottom of the Great Curry Powder Plot, returned to the fort, led by an ever smiling Ginga Don. He was mightily pleased with himself that he had alerted the monster. For that, he would be paid a bonus of ten rupees. At this rate he would soon be able to buy himself a second-hand pull-along-cab and set up in business as a tongawallah, which Westerners knew as a cab driver. He would not be content to be a fanwallah all his life, on no, sir, a thousand thousand times no.

51

Mudyard Tipling
A self portrait

THE MONSOON

It rained, and it rained, and it rained,

And it rained, and it rained and rained.

Then it rained, and it rained and it rained,

And it rained and it rained and it rained.

Then it rained some more.

Mudyard Tipling
British India, 1900

52

4

MUDYARD Tipling, posing as Mortimer Hacker of the London *Times* for an arranged interview with the quiet revolutionary Goondhi, rapped on the front door of the tiny bungalow in downtown Kalabar with the handle of his umbrella. 'Do come in,' a soft, gentle voice called from a back room. 'The door is always open except to bad spirits.'

Mortimer, alias Mudyard, fell face first through the doorway as he tripped on an unseen step.

'Mind the step,' the soft, gentle voice called.

As he stood up in what was an eerie room of dark, flickering shadows, Mudyard cracked his head against an ornamental oil lamp hanging from the ceiling and fell back to his knees.

'Mind your head on the oil lamp,' the soft, gentle voice called.

Mudyard crawled forwards on all fours to make sure he missed the lamp when he stood up, and as he scurried across the thick Indian rug he trapped his right hand in a mousetrap that had been placed in the middle of the room.

'Mind the mousetrap,' the soft, gentle voice called.

As he wrestled the mousetrap off his hand, Mortimer, trying to control the tears of pain rolling down his cheeks, kicked a bucket that was catching rainwater coming through a leaking roof as the monsoon at last abated. The bucket tipped over and soaked the white cotton trousers of the lightweight suit he had ordered specially from a London tailor for his European businessman disguises.

'Mind the water bucket,' the soft, gentle voice called.

Mudyard was sitting squeezing the water out of his trousers when there was a growl, and out of the shadows came a small black and white fox terrier that fixed its teeth into his right ankle. As he prodded the dog with his umbrella and pulled his bruised and bleeding ankle away his right trouser leg split at the knee.

'Beware of the dog,' the soft, gentle voice called.

Placing the bucket over the dog, Mudyard got up and limped without any more mishap towards the voice coming from an adjoining room.

He peered through the gloom to find a wizened little nut-brown man sitting cross-legged on a mat in the middle of the floor wearing, as he had anticipated, nothing but a small sheet.

Mudyard bowed in respectful greeting. 'Mortimer Hacker of the London *Times*,' he announced.

'I am afraid there is nobody of that name here,' the soft, gentle voice said.

'No, I am he,' said Mortimer, laughing lightly at the misunderstanding. 'We have an appointment, Mr Goondhi.'

'Goondhi?' said the soft, gentle voice. 'Oh, you want the house opposite. I am Goondha, the grocer.'

Mortimer made his apologies, and on his way out had his left trouser leg torn by the terrier and fell up the step and out of the door.

'Mind the step,' the soft, gentle voice said.

The real Goondhi greeted him on his porch with the palms of his hands placed together, the fingers close to his lips, and with a slow, reverential bow as if he was studying Mortimer's shoes.

'Excuse my dishevelled appearance,' said Mudyard, alias Mortimer. 'I had a run-in with a dog in Goondha's house across the road.'

'Ah, my Uncle Akbar,' said Goondhi. 'Always the aggressive one in the family.'

'Goondha the grocer is your uncle?' said Mudyard.

'Oh no,' said Goondhi. 'Akbar the terrier.'

He looked at Mudyard's torn, soaking trousers. 'It is not what you wear on the outside but how you feel and act here on the inside that matters,' Goondhi said, tapping a slim hand against his heart and then straightening the white sheet that ran diagonally down from his left shoulder. It was gathered and tucked neatly around the middle of his otherwise naked body that was as slim as a sapling.

'A thousand and one pardons for the mix up. The home of Goondha. The home of Goondhi. It is easy for the tongawallahs to confuse the two.'

He invited Mudyard into his tiny, spartan, three-roomed bungalow in which there was not room to swing a sporran. Mudyard was given a small cane chair in which to sit, while Goondhi sat cross-legged on a cushion.

'I am ashamed to say that I am not on speaking terms with the grocer Goondha at the moment,' Goondhi said. 'I usually preach tolerance, understanding and, most important, dialogue, but he has stretched my forbearance to breaking point by setting a mousetrap that could easily harm my furry little cousin Dilip.'

The throbbing pain in Mudyard's blue-bruised right hand made him silently wish that Dilip had got to the trap before he arrived.

'It is my belief that no creature should ever be treated with anything less than equality. This is what we would all expect in the life hereafter, so why not here now?'

Mudyard arranged his face in what he hoped was a look of sympathetic understanding and not complete bewilderment.

'Please forgive my bad manners in not offering you a cup of tea or anything to eat,' said Goondhi. 'It is just that I do not have any such things in my home. They are too great a temptation when I am in the middle of a twenty-eight day fast.'

Mudyard was aware of his stomach rumbling. It was at least four hours since he had been fed a full English breakfast.

'I am immensely honoured and privileged that a man from the world-renowned *Times* of London should deem it appropriate to come and interview me,' said Goondhi, knowing full well, thanks to Ginga Don's infallible listening service, that he was talking to the disguised British agent Mudyard Tipling.

Mudyard, convinced that Goondhi had fallen for his cover story, took a notebook and pencil from his pocket. 'We know that you have a growing influence as a leader of many, what shall I say, ordinary Indian folk,' said Mudyard, 'and my Editor has requested that I get your views on the future of this great country.'

'Let me first of all correct you on a very important point,' said Goondhi. 'For a start, there is no such thing as *ordinary* Indian folk, nor indeed ordinary human beings or creatures of any kind. They are all extraordinary, and none should be treated as being more or less ordinary than the other. As for the future of this great country, that is in the lap of the gods. It could be decided, for instance, by Akbar whom you have already met.'

He pointed at a bird hopping on the window sill. 'Or perhaps it could be my mother there,' he said, then indicating a beetle crossing the floor, 'or even my great-grandfather Vikramsinha, the beetle.'

'You refer to all these creatures as relatives,' said Mudyard.

'That is so,' said Goondhi, happily playing the weird eccentric that he knew was the Western view of him. 'In the world that I believe in with all my heart and soul nobody dies but passes on to a new existence, returning to earth in another form. This is why I would never harm a fly. Who knows, it could be your sister. We are all of God and we are all God. Our bodies are our temples, and we must worship them.'

Goondhi smiled inwardly as he watched Mudyard noting down the nonsense in which he only partly believed.

'You have had an English education,' said Mudyard. 'How did you reconcile yourself to living in England when you hold beliefs so diametrically opposed to those held in the Motherland?'

'Your society is not so much different to Indian

society, and so I felt quite at home while studying at Cambridge University,' he said. 'You have a class system, with the poor getting poorer, the rich getting richer and the people in the middle working furiously to try to go up and to stop going down. You also have your Untouchables – the football hooligans. It is a society with which I hold no brief, and I abhor it as much as the unfair and unjust Raj system encouraged by the British. My belief, and this is the future for India and possibly even England – although that is highly improbable – is that everybody should be equal, none more equal than others.'

Mudyard decided to steer the interview to the point he really wanted to discuss. 'You studied English history while at Cambridge,' he said.

'Indeed I did,' said Goondhi, reaching into his memory for meaningful dates. 'There was the Battle of Hastings 1066, Thomas Becket appallingly murdered on the Catheral steps at Canterbury 1170, Henry the Fifth triumphant at Agincourt 1415 thanks to the yeoman of England, Drake sinks the Spanish Armada 1588, and Guy Fawkes gallantly tries to blow up Parliament in the Great Gunpowder Plot of 1605.'

Mudyard felt a tingle of excitement. He had strayed into the territory that he wanted to explore. 'You, uh sympathised with Guy Fawkes?' he asked casually.

'Did not every sane English person outside the Establishment?' said Goondhi, thoroughly enjoying himself. 'Would the vast majority not have liked to have seen him succeed with the plot to get rid of the building that represented all that was corrupt in the world?'

58

Having established that Guy Fawkes was his inspiration, Mudyard now skilfully brought the subject round to embrace India. 'Could you, uh, see a similar plot working here in India?' Mudyard asked as subtly as possible so as not to raise Goondhi's suspicions.

'What a splendid idea,' said Goondhi. 'Who would have thought that the man from the *Times* would have had such devious thoughts.'

Now Mudyard was embarrassed. 'Goodness me,' he said, 'I am not suggesting it for one minute. I am merely enquiring about the possibility, or even the probability, of something like it happening here in India.'

'Of course you are,' said Goondhi, now swinging the interview around so that he was the one asking the questions. 'And exactly what sort of plot do you have in mind?'

'Well, the Great Gunpowder Plot by Guy Fawkes and his collaborators failed,' said Mudyard, 'so I was wondering about you perhaps trying a Great Curry Powder Plot.'

Goondhi clapped his hands together in fabricated excitement. 'Wonderful!' he exclaimed. 'So inventive. But how would it work? Who on earth would be the targets?'

'Well,' said Mudyard, warming to the idea, 'you would first of all need to collect and collate great reserves of curry powder.'

'That is not easily done,' said Goondhi, 'but it is a mere problem of logistics. Pray carry on outlining your ingenious plot.'

'Well,' continued Mudyard, 'you would then find a

way of getting it into the food of the British troops and Government officials who are virtually running India.'

'Ruining India, I would say.'

'The hard part will be getting it into the cook houses at the well-guarded forts and barracks.'

'True,' said Goondhi. 'So how do you suggest that we should do that?'

'How about by tunnelling in under the cook houses and government houses and bringing the curry in through a network of underground tunnels?'

'Quite astonishing. But how are we going to guarantee that the curry is eaten?'

'That's easy,' said Mudyard, his inventive writer's mind racing away. 'Nearly every week in India there is a different festival to honour this god or that god. You tell the Viceroy of India that the Curry God is to be honoured on such-and-such a day when everybody in India must have a curry dinner or risk the curse of the Curry God coming down on his head, or, more accurately, his stomach.'

'But what is the point of making all the soldiers and British officials eat the curry?' asked Goondhi mischievously.

'It will be a particularly strong flavour and much too hot for sensitive British stomachs,' said Mudyard. 'They will all be struck down with Curryitis, and the soldiers will be too weak to fight and the officials too weak to negotiate. You will then demand their withdrawal from India, and they will be only too happy to hurry home to get some good old British roast beef and Yorkshire pudding down them. And there you have it. The British

India Empire brought down without a shot being fired or a sword being raised.'

'That is a most splendid plot,' said Goondhi, applauding. 'I wish I had thought of it.'

'Thought of what?' said Mudyard.

'The Great Curry Powder Plot.'

'So you admit that you know of its existence?' said Mudyard triumphantly.

'But of course, said Goondhi. 'You have just told me about it.'

Mudyard was confused. 'No,' he said, 'I have just interviewed you on the subject.'

'I think,' said Goondhi, 'that when you read your notes back you will find that the Great Curry Powder Plot is your idea, and a very good one it is too. I will see to it that you get the full credit to which you are entitled. In fact, I shall write a letter to the *Times*.'

Goondhi's eyes turned towards the door. 'Oh hello, father,' he said. 'I'm so glad you could join us. Come and meet the distinguished journalist Mr Mortimer Hacker, of the London *Times*.'

Mortimer, alias Mudyard, stood up and prepared to greet Goondhi's father with an outstretched hand. He then froze with horror. Slithering towards him from under the door was the biggest cobra he had ever clapped eyes on.

He had previously seen Indian cobras only in baskets hawked around by snake charmers, and if they came within twenty yards of him he felt physically sick and muscle-bound. Now he was *rigor mortis* stiff.

Goondhi raised an arm, and the cobra lifted its huge,

dilating hood of a head and came into an almost upright position just feet away from the comatose Mudyard.

'He's so pleased to see you,' said Goondhi. 'It is not often we get visitors from Europe. There was an unfortunate incident with the last one, a tax official called Ponsonby-Smith. He reacted rather aggressively when father joined us and tried to hit poor Daddy with his umbrella. Extremely deplorable manners I thought. I'm afraid that Father rather over-reacted and bit him. He can be quite venomous, can Daddy, and the unfortunate man was dead within thirty seconds.'

Raising a finger of admonishment at the cobra, Goondhi waggled his head from side to side. 'That was very, very naughty of you, Daddy.'

The cobra hung its head in shame.

'But it was quite understandable in the circumstances,' said Goondhi, 'so don't feel too badly about it.'

The cobra lifted its head, and seemed almost ready to smile.

'Let's face it,' added Goondhi, 'Mr Ponsonby-Smith over-taxed himself with his umbrella and paid the supreme price. All tax men should heed the warning, or risk the cobra's revenge. But Mr Ponsonby-Smith has since forgiven my father, and has often come to visit us in his new existence as a horned lizard.'

Goondhi realised that Mudyard, still standing stock still as though suddenly turned to stone, seemed just a little apprehensive. 'You don't have to worry about Daddy,' he said. 'Provided you don't make any sudden movements and, of course, keep your umbrella out of his sight, you are perfectly safe in his company.'

Mudyard sank very, very slowly back into the cane chair, ensuring that his buttocks covered the umbrella and kept it hidden from the cobra's gaze. The point of the umbrella was, so to speak, stuck up his Khyber, but this was no time for fidgeting. Breathing was the only luxury he would allow himself.

As Goondhi waved his arms around, the cobra jiggled from side to side while still in an upright position. 'Look, Daddy's dancing,' said Goondhi. 'That's his way of showing you that you are a welcome guest in the house. You might find this hard to believe, but he can hit any unwelcome guests between the eyes with his venom from a distance of ten feet.'

Mudyard was quite happy to accept this as fact without trying to put it to the test. The cobra seemed to tire of dancing, and came to a rest curled around Mudyard's feet.

'Poor Daddy's quite exhausted,' explained Goondhi. 'He's been travelling around the country entertaining people with his solo dancing. He is leading a campaign to have all cobras released from those suffocating baskets. They do not need to be cramped into baskets, or to have those cheating charmers pretending to make them dance with their musical instruments. Did you know that cobras, all snakes for that matter, are deaf to high frequencies, and that they dance to the rhythm of the charmer's pipe movements not his music?'

Mudyard blinked his staring eyes in response. It was the only part of his body he dared move.

Goondhi got up from his cushion and lifted the cobra

off Mudyard's feet. 'Come on, Daddy,' he said. 'You're being rude lying on Mr Hacker's feet. I'll put you on my bed but only on the understanding that you let me have it back when it is time for me to sleep. I find it most uncomfortable having to spend all night on my cushion.'

When Goondhi returned from his bedroom he found Mudyard at the front door.

'It's been, uh, a delight to have met you and your, um, family, Mr Goondhi,' he said. 'I must dash now. Have to file my copy to London. Thank you for a very interesting interview, and please give my kindest regards to Mr Goondhi Senior.'

'Oh, the pleasure was all mine,' said Goondhi, smiling and bowing, with his hands in the pressed together position. 'It was extremely enlightening, and I thank you most profusely for the idea of the Great Curry Powder Plot. That is worth careful consideration.'

As Mudyard stepped out on to the porch, Goondhi beckoned him. 'One thing I forgot to mention,' he said, 'is that while you are on a reporting assignment here in Kalabar I recommend that you try to interview our local teller of tales. Mudyard Tipling is his name. He knows everything about everything and could tell you much more about the Great Curry Powder Plot than I ever could. As an obviously educated man, you may perhaps while interviewing him give him some lessons about cadence and scanning.'

Mudyard was on the point of protesting most vehemently, but then remembered that he was Mortimer

Hacker. 'I too have heard about this Mudyard Tipling,' said Mudyard, 'and by all accounts he is a ballad-poet potentially in the class of the esteemed Rudyard Kipling.'

'That is a matter of opinion,' said Goondhi, smiling. 'Only somebody who is not blessed with an ear and an eye for poetry would say such a thing. Goodbye now, Mr Hacker. Have a pleasant journey home to London, and thanks once again for the idea of the intriguing Great Curry Powder Plot.'

It was a thoroughly confused Mudyard who walked away from Goondhi's house to call a tongawallah. And it was a thoroughly satisfied Goondhi who waved him away. Confusion was exactly what he had meant to cause.

As Mudyard prepared to climb on to the tongawallah's customised three-wheel bike, the fox terrier came and claimed what was left of his right trouser leg. 'Go away, Akbar,' growled Mudyard, 'or I'll set Mr Goondhi Senior on to you.'

The monster sat on the cane chair vacated by Mudyard in Goondhi's meditation room, the cobra curled up on his lap.

'Did you learn anything from Mudyard Tipling?' he asked, 'apart from the fact that he's the most moronic secret agent since the Burpa spy who disguised himself as a tiger in the middle of the hunting season. His head is still mounted on the wall at the Khasi's palace.'

'All that I learned is that they have not the slightest idea of how we are going to put the Great Curry

Powder Plot into operation,' said Goondhi. 'That stupid man Mudyard did not manage to get a single fact out of me, and I saw to it that he did most of the talking. He finished up virtually interviewing himself.'

The monster, maskless because Goondhi was the only man alive who knew who he was, laughed. 'We will soon rid India of British rule,' he said, 'because Mudyard typifies their stupidity.'

'What have they ever done for this great country?' asked Goondhi.

'You mean apart from bringing to an end the reign of the barbaric Moghul empire,' said the monster in a clearly English-educated voice, 'abolishing widow burning, building roads, railway networks and an electric telegraph system and setting up an education structure? Not a lot.'

'Yes, and all done for their benefit rather than ours,' said Goondhi. 'Roads and trains to improve the business prospects to make British companies richer, and an education system that cuts at the very heart of the Indian way of life, questioning our culture and, more serious still, our religions. Queen Victoria has been proclaimed Empress of India, but what does she know of our country and our traditions? It is a travesty and must come to an end.'

'I agree wholeheartedly with you Brother Goondhi,' said the monster, 'and it will be sooner rather than later. I can report that the Great Curry Powder operation is progressing satisfactorily, and we should be in a position to launch it within the month.'

'I hear from Ginga Don that you had quite a triumph

over the Burpas this week,' said Goondhi.

'Yes, you could say that I scorched the pants off them,' said the monster. 'They had captured a patrol of thirteen soldiers from the Foot and Mouth regiment, and were holding them in a cave at the Khyber Pass. I frightened them off with a few well-aimed belches of flame.'

'Where on earth did you learn to throw flame in such a spectacular fashion?' Goondhi asked.

'It was an art taught to me by my father, who used to earn a living in the London markets as a fire-eater,' said the monster. 'It is amazing what you can achieve with a flask of paraffin, a match and a lot of puff. I can get quite fired up, I can tell you.'

'It is to the stomachs of the British that we must bring the great vindaloo fire,' said Goondhi.

The cobra raised its head and nodded.

'Don't worry, Father,' said Goondhi. 'We will soon have our Independence.'

Mudyard Tipling
A self portrait

AN INDEPENDENT MAN

A wise old Indian wanted independence
Without having to show condescendence.
So in great secrecy he planned and plotted
How he could make the Brits get knotted.
He told the man from the London *Times*
That they would pay for their crimes
By first of all losing their minds,
Then having a volcano up their behinds.

Mudyard Tipling
British India,1900

5

THE monsoon season had been and gone, but still Sir Sidney Ruff-Diamond was left feeling high and dry about the Great Curry Powder Plot. That moron Mudyard Tipling had come back from his interview with Goondhi full of excitement about having uncovered their strategy, but under close cross-examination he confessed that he had been cleverly duped into giving his imagined version rather than garnering the real plans.

Sir Sidney had called an emergency council of non-violent war at Government House. Present were Captain Ffortescue-Ffortescue, Sergeant-Major Thomas, a contrite Mudyard Tipling and, representing the local mission, Brother Barnes Belcher, who had recently resurfaced after he had disappeared following a scandal at the harem when he had literally been caught by the Khasi of Kalabar with his trousers down. He assured everybody that he had come back a new man, with a much clearer vision of his role in bringing hope and salvation to the lives of ordinary Indians who did not have the great wealth of the Khasis of this unjust world.

Also present, of course, with his ears working overtime, was the faithful fanwallah Ginga Don. He had set up five fans and was energetically working each one of them, bringing hand-driven air-conditioning to the oppressively hot conference room.

'Somewhere,' Sir Sidney said to Captain Ffortescue-Ffortescue, opening the meeting after a sixth cup of gin, 'there have to be great flippin' stockpiles of curry powder. What progress have your men made in finding it?'

'Fo sar there have not been any signs of quarge launtities of curry,' said Ffortescue-Ffortescue, fiddling with the bandage covering his still tender nose following his heat-exhaustion fall. 'More than pifty fatrols have searched within a mundred hile radius, and we have hit a wank blall.'

Sir Sidney wished he had never asked. He turned to Sergeant-Major Thomas. 'Anything further to report, Sergeant-Major – preferably in the Queen's English?' he asked, taking a sip of neat gin from his finest English bone china tea cup.

'I doubts very much if we is going to 'ave hany luck tracking it down, sir,' said Doubting Thomas, his parade ground voice booming around the room, the entire house and the grounds. Ginga Don's ears turned red with the sudden assault.

'Sorry to interrupt you, Sergeant-Major,' said Sir Sidney, shouting to make himself heard, 'but we are still trying to keep this matter a secret. Would you mind bringing the volume down?'

'Sorry, sir, force of 'abit,' said the Sergeant-Major in a whisper that still made Ginga Don's fan quiver. 'They is very crafty, whoever our henemy is, sir. We did find one mountain of powder 'idden in the back yard of a notorious agitator. When my boyhos set fire to it, as was agreed, it turned out to be gunpowder. My boyhos are recovering in the local 'ospital.'

'And what was this I heard about your confrontation with the revolting Burpas?'

'Yes, sir, I 'as made a full report to the Captain,' said the Sergeant-Major. 'We was caught hunawares by the Burpas when taking shelter from the shower what was wetter than what we hexpected. Bunghit Don, the rebel leader and a nasty bit of work if you asks me, gave us a message that he is not the slightest bit hinterested in peace negotiations. He was about to hexecute hus, sir, when a sort of Welsh dragon came into the cave breathing fire. The scaredy cat Burpas ran hoff, and I led my boyhos to safety with the help of this fanwallah here, who was worried that we might 'ave been drowned.'

Sir Sidney reached into his pocket and took out a handful of several hundred rupees, and gave two of them to Ginga Don. 'Well done, Gingy-Thingy,' he said. 'Here's a reward. Now can you get my fan working just a bit faster on my right side. It's like a bloody furnace in here.'

Ginga pocketed the two rupees while salaaming, listening and working the five fans faster all at the same time.

'As a matter of interest, Brother Sergeant-Major,' said Brother Belcher, 'how did you manage to escape from the dragon?'

'I stared him down, sir,' said the Sergeant-Major. 'It was no different than facing the Pontypool front row. I just stood my ground and 'e turned tail and ran off. It was a bit 'airy for some of my boyhos, but they 'as not 'ad the benefit of 'aving been brought hup in the Valleys where men is men and the sheep is worried.'

Brother Belcher shook his head in wonder. 'I greatly

71

admire your bravery, Sergeant-Major,' he said. 'If that had been me in the same situation I would have prayed for divine intervention.'

'And while you were on your knees, if you will forgive me for saying, sir,' said the Sergeant-Major, 'you would 'ave been turned into burnt toast. You would not 'ave 'ad a prayer.'

'Did you get the feeling that the Burpas might be behind the Great Curry Powder Plot, Sergeant-Major?' asked gin-sodden Sir Sidney.

'Most definitely not, sir,' said the Sergeant-Major emphatically. 'They 'as heard the rumours of the plot, but they is completely and utterly opposed to anything non-violent. All they is interested in is a bloody good war.'

Sir Sidney took another sip of gin. 'I don't know,' he said, shaking his head, 'we're no nearer getting to the bottom of it. I've tipped off the Viceroy about the plot, and he has ordered a round-the-clock watch on the kitchens of all government employees and on army cook houses. What do you hear on your rounds, Brother Belcher?'

'I, too, have heard the rumours,' said Brother Belcher, staring at his palms to see if there were any signs there to help him see what was going to happen. 'My only concern is that there should be no bloodshed on either side. I would much rather they were planning a Great Curry Powder Plot than a Great Gunpowder Plot. Many of the Indians I talk to are hell bent, excuse the phrase, on getting rid of the British influence in their country by fair means or foul. To paraphrase a famous quote that will be used one day, 'Guns make you powerful, curry makes you fart.'*

Belcher had been working as a missionary in Kalabar for ten years after carrying out similar duties in the East End of his native London. Educated at Cambridge University and at the Sorbonne in Paris, he had studied Indian languages and religions. One of the gifts he had acquired while mixing with the wise men of the mystical east was an ability to know what would be happening years ahead, although only time would tell that he was not quite one hundred per cent tuned in to the future as he thought. He could read palms, playing cards, tea leaves, the stars, crystal balls, but who in the present would have known that it was not always with anything quite like complete accuracy?

His major problem was, in fact, handling the present. He had been regarded as a likely leader of all the missions in India until he fell to the temptations of the Khasi's harem. This experience had totally confused him, and he had abandoned his previous shaky celibate calling and now preached and practised polygamy for all he was worth.

'What I learn from my daily rounds is that the average Indian in the street wants no part of British rule in their country,' Brother Belcher said, 'and the British are putting their heads in the noose by interfering with their lives. The government hold up Queen Victoria, Empress of India...'

'God Bless her,' said Ginga Don.

*'Guns make you powerful, butter makes you fat.' - Herman Goering, Nazi Reichsmarschall 1936.

73

'...as a figurehead for Indians when she is as foreign to them as the Man in the Moon. They are given portraits of her to hang on their walls, but since the Bloody, pardon my language, Mutiny of 1857 was so brutally put down she is quietly held up to ridicule and called The Hanging Lady.'

He stared into the tea leaves at the bottom of his cup. 'I can see the future here,' he said, 'and it is an India without Queens, Kings, Princes, Maharajahs, Nawabs and Khasis... and without the British.'

Sir Sidney stared into the bottom of his gin. 'Don't make me laugh,' he said. 'Next you'll be telling us that there will be a British Empire without India, Canada, South Africa, Australia and New Zealand, and Hong Kong will have gone back to the Chinese.'

'That is exactly what I see Brother Sir Sidney,' said Brother Belcher, double checking with a miniature crystal ball that he always carried around with him. 'And sooner than you think. There will be two terrible wars engulfing the whole of the world, and out of them will come a free India. Bankrupt Britain will be forced to choose between becoming the 50th State of the United States of America or a satellite of Europe, governed from Berlin. There will be an invasion of Britain through a tunnel secretly built underneath the English Channel, and London will be ransacked by an army known as Tourists.'

Mudyard Tipling stopped writing his latest poem to tune into the conversation.

'And pray, Brother Belcher, what do your tea leaves say about my reputation as a writer?' he asked. 'How

74

will I be remembered in the literary world?'

'It says here,' said Belcher, looking closer into the cup, 'that they will be saying, "Mudyard Who?".'

'But when will they be saying that?' said Mudyard.

'Next month,' said Brother Belcher crushingly. He, too, abhorred Tipling's tales and considered him as much an impostor as he himself had become as a Christian missionary. He had secretly converted to Islam, but was still taking his monthly pay cheque from the Lancastrian religious order that had sent him to India after he had got romantically involved with a Bishop's wife. They were found crossing each other in the vestry.

'Does it say anything in your lea teaves or your brystal call about future trethods of mavel?' asked the fascinated Ffortescue-Ffortescue.

'I thinks what the Captain means, begging your pardon for sticking my nose in, Captain, is future methods of travel,' said the Sergeant-Major.

'That's what I sust jaid,' said the Captain, who had talked his reverse language ever since getting hit on the back of the head by a cricket ball in a match against the Zulus during a break in the Boer War. The Zulus won by an innings and 476 runs. Or, as the Captain put it as the last British Army wicket fell, 'Mugger be, we've been zicked by the Lulus.'

'Even as we speak,' said Brother Belcher, 'there are two inventors in America called the Wrong Brothers who are working on a machine that will fly. They have managed to get it off the ground, but have yet to work out how to make it land. Everybody will be flying around one day soon on things called credit cards.'

'I think your tea leaves have become crossed,' said Sir Sidney. 'You would be much better off studying the bottom of a gin glass.'

'I have another prediction to make,' added Brother Belcher, as he tipped the leaves out into the palm of his hand. 'I see that it is the Royals who will one day lead the way in showing that you do not have to stay with the same partner all your life. A new phrase will become accepted – "to put it about a bit." And I further predict that there will be a saying that will become commonplace, "A wife is not just for Christmas".'

Sir Sidney blew his nose to disguise the fact that he was upset about the mention of wives; it had made him think specifically of his wife, and he did not even have her with him the previous Christmas. 'Can you please try to get back to the main point of today's crisis meeting, Brother,' he said, 'which is the Great Curry Wife Plot.'

He did not even realise what he had said.

'I believe you mean the Great Curry Powder Plot, Brother Sir Sidney,' said Belcher.

'That's what I said,' snapped Sir Sidney.

'I'm afraid not, Brother. You mentioned your wife, and we all sympathise with you in losing her to that despicable man, the Khasi of Kalabar.'

'I have *not* lost her,' said Sir Sidney, going down a road that he had always marked private. 'I have merely temporarily loaned her to the Khasi while she helps him get his house in order. She will return.'

'I certainly pray so, Brother Sir Sidney,' said Brother Belcher. 'Her place is here by your side.'

The Captain, the Sergeant-Major, Mudyard Tipling

76

and Ginga Don all nodded their heads in agreement.

'But how can I compete with a man who has his vast riches?' said Sir Sidney, the gin loosening his tongue more than he would have wanted. 'He has got more wealth than even Queen Victoria...'

'God Bless her,' said Ginga Don.

'...and, rumour has it, he has buried treasure that is worth more than all the Crown Jewels put together.'

'It is not the depth of your pocket that will win your wife back,' said Brother Belcher, 'but the depth of your feelings. You must convey to her exactly how you feel.'

'But how?' pleaded Sir Sidney, sinking the last mouthful of neat gin.

'By prayer,' said Brother Belcher.

'By poetry,' said Mudyard Tipling.

'By serenading her,' said the Sergeant-Major.

'By fanning her,' said Ginga Don.

'By a micket cratch,' said the Captain.

All heads turned in the direction of Ffortescue-Ffortescue.

'What did you say?' said Sir Sidney. 'What the hell is a micket cratch?'

'A came of gricket,' said the Captain, sudden excitement in his eyes. 'It's a really clever wain brave, even if I say it myself.'

'Well nobody else could,' said Sir Sidney. 'What are you talking about?'

'I think what the Captain means, begging your pardon for sticking my nose in, Captain,' said the Sergeant-Major, 'is a game of cricket.'

'But how can a game of bloody cricket get my wife

back?' spluttered Sir Sidney.

'When I was at cilitary mollege at Sandhurst,' explained the Captain, 'one of our officers wost his life to a bounder at Currey Sounty Clicket Crub. He challenged him to a distol puel, but the pricketer was a cacifist who said he would play a game of wicket for his crife.'

'Now just stop there for a minute,' said Sir Sidney, pouring himself another cupful of gin. 'Let me see if I've got this right. You're telling me that an officer at Sandhurst lost his wife to a Surrey cricketer, challenged him to a duel but then agreed to play a game of cricket for his wife?'

'That's what I sust jaid,' said the Captain. 'We got a first-class Tandhurst seam together, and seat Burrey by rine nuns, and the officer got his bife wack.'

'So you're saying that I should challenge the Khasi to a game of cricket?' said Sir Sidney, the gin parting him from what little sense that he had. 'What a great idea. I could turn my arm over to good effect once until I discovered it was much more satisfactory to get my leg over. Yes, it's a bloody good idea. What d'you think Brother Belcher?'

'I do believe it is the sort of challenge that would appeal to his ego,' said Brother Belcher. 'The man is a born gambler, and I see here in my tea leaves that it is all of sixty years before India start beating the hell – pardon my language – out of the English at cricket. One fact for which I do not have to look into the tea leaves is that the cowardly Khasi would much prefer a cricket match to a duel.'

'Him and me both,' mumbled Sir Sidney. 'But I wonder how my wife would react?'

'What woman would not want to have two men fighting over her, even if it is in something of a metaphoric sense,' said Mudyard.

'What do you think, Sergeant-Major?' said Sir Sidney, the subject of his wife now having superseded the Great Curry Powder Plot as the main item on the meeting agenda.

'Speaking personally as a Welshman from the Valleys, sir,' he said, 'I would much rather you challenged him to a game of rugby. But if it's to be cricket then I can help you get a powerful team together by bringing in some of my boyhos. They is great at playing with their balls, sir. Winners of the regimental cricket and football championships, we is sir. Mind you, we was the only regiment that entered because the others were away fighting.'

Sir Sidney got up unsteadily from his chair and walked to his desk. He wrote a letter to the Khasi with the help of Mudyard, who insisted on making it rhyme...

I CHALLENGE YOU TO A CRICKET GAME OF YOUR LIFE
WITH THE PRIZE FOR THE VICTOR MY LOVELY WIFE.
THE TEAM WHO GETS MOST RUNS IN ONE INNINGS
WILL CARRY HER OFF AS THE CAPTAIN'S WINNINGS.
WHAT SAY YOU, SIR?
OR WOULD YOU RATHER A SABRE DUEL, YOU CUR?
YOURS FRATERNALLY,
SIR SIDNEY RUFF-DIAMOND,
HER MAJESTY'S GOVERNOR OF KALABAR

Sir Sidney placed the letter in an official British India government envelope and handed it to Ginga Don. 'Guard this with your life, Gingamejig,' he said. 'Make sure it gets into the hands of the Khasi personally.'

'Yes, oh mighty one of the government of Her Majesty Queen Victoria, God Bless her,' he said. 'I will have it in the hands of the Khasi before you can say Kurmar Shri Ranjitsinhji.'

'What is he on about?' growled Sir Sidney. 'Is there nobody round here who can make sense any more?'

Ginga Don had gone like the wind before Brother Belcher could explain just who Ranjitsinhji was. 'He just happens to be the greatest cricketer that ever breathed, and is the WG Grace of India, only better,' he said. 'He followed me up to Cambridge and now Captains Sussex and plays regularly for England. He is the star player in the Khasi's team, and averages three thousand runs every season.'

'He plays for the Khasi?' Sir Sidney said, almost choking. 'Why the hell didn't you say that before I sent that letter off.'

'But you didn't ask me,' said Belcher. 'And, anyway, I thought *everybody* knew who Ranjitsinhji was."

'He is like a God here in India,' said Mudyard, who started to clear his throat. 'I've written a poem about him...'

'We've got much more important things to discuss

'The Great Ranjitsinhji played 15 Tests for England, and starred for Cambridge University and Sussex. He later became a commissioner to the League of Nations. He scored 24,692 runs at an average 56.37 during his career from 1893 to 1920. He was known as 'Smith' at university.

than your bloody poetry,' said Sir Sidney, now really ratty as well as rat-arsed. He realised he had made a challenge that he could not expect to win, not if the Khasi had the great Ranwhateverhisnamewas on his side.

Her Ladyship had suddenly become The Ashes in his life, and the Khasi was a hot favourite to retain her.

He decided he had better get the meeting back to the original main subject, as the Great Curry Powder Plot could make everything elementary.

'We are keeping a close watch on a revolutionary called Goondhi, Brother Belcher,' said Sir Sidney. 'Have you ever come across him?'

Belcher was about to answer when the grandfather clock in the corner of the room struck twelve times. 'Goodness me,' he said, 'is that the time. I'm afraid I must dash away to carry out some urgent missionary work. I should have gone an hour ago. I am showing examples of English farming techniques to some Indian farmwallahs. One day they will be able to watch it on a new system called Smellyvision.'

'For a man who is alwaysh looking into the future,' said Sir Sidney after Brother Belcher had departed, 'I just wish he would make more of an effort to find out where he ish shupposed to be in the here and now.'

He drained his cup, and realised he had over indulged when he found himself peering at two Captains, two Sergeant-Majors and, God help us, two Mudyard Tiplings, who were blurred figures looking back at him.

'I'm going to adjourn the resht of the meeting,' he slurred. 'We will discush the Great Cricket Powder Plot another time. I now want you to put all your thoughtsh into helping me find a winning cricket team. Thish ish not an ordinary cricket match. Thish ish war.'

'I shall organise some tricket tials just as soon as we get fack to the bort,' said the Captain. 'I rather gancy a fame myself.'

Sir Sidney would not have understood what he was talking about even if he had been awake. He was asleep with his head on the mahogany conference table, dreaming of his wife wielding a cricket bat and hitting the Khasi's balls all over the field.

The Khasi of Kalabar dropped into the deepest of deep depressions when he read the Governor's Ginga-delivered letter. It put him in an impossible no-win situation. His pride would plead that he should accept the challenge. The cricket gods would never forgive him if he turned down a cricket match. The game had become a religion in India since they had picked it up from British soldiers. It was one of the few decent things the British had brought to his country, that and Yorkshire pudding for which he had developed an all-devouring appetite.

He could not possibly throw the match because that would just not be cricket. His ego demanded that he should go all out to win the game, and he would never be able to look his subjects in the face again if he were to lose, particularly with the legendary Ranjitsinhji in his side.

They were all the positive things. The negative one that stuck in his stomach like a dagger point was the fact that victory would mean him winning Her Ladyship outright. Perhaps a sabre duel would be a better idea? No, she was not worth the sacrifice of his life, and fencing was not his forte. But some off-the-wrist spinning, that was a different matter altogether.

Her Ladyship was causing more disruption in his life than ever. No sooner had he given in to the demands for housekeeping than he was faced by another delegation of wives. This time they had given him an ultimatum: allow us each a night out every week 'with the girls' or we will again withdraw your humping and grunting rights.

Her Ladyship, of course, was behind it. He had tried telling her that there was a plot to burn her insides out with curry powder in the hope that it would convince her that she should sail home to England. But it just added to her determination to stay with him. 'You have the power and the wherewithal to protect me, Khasi-wasi,' she had said. 'I know that I am safe while I am here with you. In return I shall look after you, organise you and your wives, and make sure that you have everything you need when you need it. Everything but humping and grunting. You cannot have that until you allow your wives the time they need to pursue leisure interests away from the palace.'

The Khasi was being slowly and systematically smothered and suffocated by her. He had seen it happen to husbands in England while studying there, and used to regularly thank the gods of love that he did not have to go along with any of that one man, one wife nonsense. Yet here he was being treated like a henpecked husband by a lady who was not even one of his wives. Could he, would he, deliberately lose a cricket match to get rid of her?

It was tempting, but the thought of victory over the British on the cricket field was too much of a magnet.

Her Ladyship found out about her husband's letter within five minutes of it being handed to the Khasi. She paid the loyal Ginga Don a bonus of five rupees for the information.

She was flattered and yet at the same time frightened by the fact that a cricket match was to be played with herself as the prize for the winner. Just supposing the Khasi were to lose?

The thought of going back to poor Sidney - poor being the key word - petrified her. She had heard from Ginga Don about how he was beginning to lose himself in an alcoholic haze. He had only himself to blame. It was he who started playing around with the Khasi's harem wives, running wild like a child in a sweet shop. She had discovered the six wives whose favours he had enjoyed, and had taken revenge by making sure they were always on the Khasi's rota at their 'curse' time of the month.

Her Ladyship just wished she had paid more attention to the game of cricket when she used to go to those tea parties at Lord's while the flanelled fools ran around in the mid-day sun. She then might have better understood exactly how she was going to be won or lost.

She looked up a book of cricket laws that she found in the Khasi's study.

'The side that wins the toss,' she read, 'can choose to go in or out into the field. The side that goes in remains in until it is out, and then the side that has got them out goes in. The batsmen not batting stay in the pavilion until a batsman is out and then they go in until they are out. The bowler bowls six balls which is called an over, and when it is over another bowler bowls an over from the other end until he has finished an over. The umpire calls 'over' and then another over begins until it is over. The side scoring most runs after they have both been in and out two times wins, or it is possible for a side that has been in just once to win by an innings after putting the other side in again for a second innings immediately after their first innings. The team that stays in longest does not necessarily win because it is the amount of runs scored by the team when it is in that will decide the outcome.'

Her Ladyship had a headache by the time she had finished reading. She really did not know whether she was in or out.

Meantime the Khasi was using the British-erected telegraph system to send an urgent message to Kurmar Shri Ranitsinhji, His Highness Jam Saheb of Nawanagir and of Sussex and England. It read:

COME IMMEDIATELY STOP BRING YOUR BAT AND HUNDREDS OF RUNS STOP WE ARE GOING TO KNOCK THE DEVIL OUT OF THE BRITISH STOP YOUR CAPTAIN NEEDS YOU - THE CRICKETING KHASI OF KALABAR.

The Khasi summoned his head groundsman. 'I want

85

you to prepare a slow turning wicket,' he ordered. 'I am going to tie the Governor up by the googlies.'

The cunning Khasi of Kalibar had worked it all out. Having won the cricket match against the hated British, he would be such a hero in India that no judge in the land would dare take action against him for executing Her Ladyship.

Captain Ffortescue-Ffortescue was shocked and horrifed when he arrived back at the fort to find the newly arrived Lieutenant Montague Grimcock behind one of the Fort Phucka walls trying to do unspeakable things to the regimental camel.

'Just what do you think you are louing, Dieutenant?' he demanded. 'And put your dilt kown immediately. You are cightening the framel.'

'Awfully sorry, sir, that you caught me in this embarrassing position,' the lieutenant said in a terribly posh voice that had Windsor and Eton embroidered into it, 'but I am just taking my turn.'

'Taking your turn to whoo dot?' said the Captain.

'Well I'm trying to have my way with this dashed camel, sir,' he said, 'but I haven't quite got the knack. I don't seem to be able to get stuck in, if you follow me. In fact I'm having to follow it. Every time I make a thrust she takes a pace forward. At least, I hope it's a she. I'm not the other way inclined, don't you know, although I was forced to do a little leaning against the Eton wall. We started this pantomime half a mile away over the other side of the fort.'

'What are you? Some sort of pisgusting dervert?'

'I'm only doing what all the chaps in the ranks do, sir,' said the lieutenant. 'I was feeling rather frisky and I asked them what they do for sex, and they said that they use the old camel and go to town.'

'Yes,' said the Captain. 'They cride the ramel into town and visit the bocal lothrel.'

The lieutenant blushed as red as his tunic.

'Tell me, lieutenant, can you clay pricket?'

'Oh, rather sir,' said the lieutenant. 'Got my County cap with Middlesex before I came out here, and I hit several tons against those dreadful Harrow chappies.'

'Well it's saved you from a charge of mile visconduct,' said the Captain. 'You can help me sick a pide to play for the Governor. Are you a batter or a bowler?'

'I do a bit of both, sir.'

'Sought tho,' said the Captain. 'Seeing you with that camel, I guessed you were a bit of a two-sway winger.'

Behind the far fort wall an Indian was practising his spin bowling. 'I wonder,' he thought to himself, 'who I should play for? I am sure I could have the great Ranjitsinhji in two minds. He would not know whether to hit me for a four or a six.'

He bowled a battered old ball at the unguarded wicket twenty-two strides away, and for the sixth successive time he pitched the ball two yards to the right and knocked back the middle stump.

Not for nothing was Ginga Don known in his village as the spinwallah.

Mudyard Tipling
A self portrait

THE LOSING GAME

A cricket match is to be played
For the hand of the Governor's wife.
The Khasi has already prayed
That he loses this game of his life.
He would squander a large booty
To have her taken out of his sight,
For she is hardly a beauty,
And is turning his day into night.

Mudyard Tipling
British India, 1900

6

NEWS of the cricket duel, for duel is what it was, spread like a rash, and it was the talk of India before you could say Kurmar Shri Ranjitsinhji. It was also the main subject of conversation up the Khyber Pass where rebel leader Bunghit Din, he of the newly singed bum, called a council of war – the violent kind.

The Burpas were an ancient, wandering tribe, not to be confused with the Gherkins, the Afghoons or the Kashunkaries. They had been chased out of Afghanistan by the Afghans, out of India by the Bengalis, out of Nepal by the Gerkhas and out of just about everywhere by the Moghuls. They were once trapped in the Khyber Pass by the Shortunn Kurlies, and that was the most painful experience in their long history.

It amused them to see the British soldiers and government officials celebrating the start of their twentieth century as if it was something special. The Burpas had been in existence for more than five thousand years, and Bunghit Din wanted to go down in their history books as the leader who found them a permanent home. He also wanted to be the first Burpa chief to lead them to a victory of any kind. They were troublemaking tribesmen who always started wars but never knew how to finish them.

There was nobody braver or more committed in combat than the Burpas, but they had a major problem. The excitement of war sent them into a blind ecstasy, and they would more often than not finish up fighting each other in the belief they were beating up the enemy. They invented a phrase that was one day to become well known and deeply feared in modern warfare: *friendly fire*.

One Burpa general had been decorated by the Indians for blowing up his own regimental headquarters during a battle with the Bengalis. Another had single handedly captured his own battalion and had handed them over to the enemy, himself included. Then there was the time in 1742 when they made the easily understandable error of turning right instead of left and invading Russia thinking it was the rather smaller territory of Kashmir. They got a terrible kick up the Cossacks.

Their most famous defeat had come in the Battle of the Khyber Pass in 1854 when their leaders had been bayonetted up the rear by their own troops when they bent down to pick up some stones strewn in their path by the retreating British. It was following that battle against the London Fusiliers that 'Up the Khyber Pass' entered the Cockney rhyming slang vocabulary, which was later shortened to 'Up the Khyber'.

It was their skill in shooting each other that gave rise to another saying: 'With friends like these, who needs enemies?' This self-destruct mentality was a handicap that Bunghit Din was determined to overcome, and he had spent months drilling his troops into recognising each other and getting them to accept that they were on their own side. To help them with the identification process, he came up with the clever idea of having their names printed on the backs of their uniforms (This concept was later filched by football shirt manufacturers without any credit being given to Bunghit Din as the originator of the idea). It was only after fifty thousand uniform tunics had been manufactured with the individual names printed large on the backs that some bright spark pointed out to Bunghit Din the minor fact that ninety-eight per cent of his troops were illiterate and would not be able to read the names.

But Bunghit refused to be beaten. He gave his troops a crash course in see-it-say-it word recognition, and he was now convinced he had them as ready as they ever would be for a raid on Kalabar. His eye was trained on Fort Phucka as a base to get a first foothold in India, and he sensed that the day of the great cricket match was an ideal time to launch an all-out attack.

Bunghit Din was a natural-born leader. He had taken over as chief of the Burpas from his father, Bunghit Din One, who had been an all-Asian wrestling champion. He had lost his unbeaten record in his last fight when his opponent, the famous Brown Bomber Body Bender of Bombay, had tied him in so many knots that he was rolled home from the stadium like a human hoop. He died a week later of hooping cough, and on his death bed whispered a secret to Bunghit Din Two. He revealed the hiding place of the Khasi of Kalabar's treasure, and this was an extra motivation for Bunghit Din Two to establish a bridgehead in Kalabar. Once they had taken over the fort, he planned to quietly plunder the treasure and then he would be so rich that he would not need to worry about fighting for any more land. He would buy it and become the most powerful landowner and, eventually landlord, in India.

The Burpas leader was intrigued to hear that the winner of the cricket duel would claim Her Ladyship, the British Governor of Kalabar's wife, as the prize. 'She must be a very special woman,' Bunghit Din said to his generals as they planned their assault on Fort Phucka. 'Perhaps we should consider taking her captive and holding her for ransom.'

Little did they know that the Khasi of Kalabar would willingly have paid a king's ransom to have her kidnapped, but not a single rupee to get her back.

The cricket match had been scheduled for the first day of November, and that was the date that Bunghit Din and his generals decided they would set out to overrun the fort. Bunghit hoped by then that he would be able to sit down on an unscorched behind to celebrate a return to the territory the Burpas had been forced to abandon when driven out of India by the Kashunuts one hundred and ten years earlier.

He had kept to himself the secret of the Khasi's treasure. First he would capture Fort Phucka, then kidnap Her Ladyship to see what was so special about her, and then he would dig up the treasure. If she was *that* special, perhaps he might even consider sharing it with her.

It was not only the Burpas who were planning to launch their offensive on the day of the cricket duel. The Great Curry Powder Plot plotters were deciding on exactly the same course of action. They had codenamed it VD Day, for Vindaloo Day.

'This is an ideal opportunity to catch out the British

92

while their minds are on other matters,' said the quiet revolutionary Goondhi, with the monster sitting nodding his approval in the background. 'We will strike while they have their eye on the cricket.'

He was addressing a meeting of the ten committee men who would start off a carefully choreographed chain reaction that would sweep across India at the speed of sound. The secret was to be passed along on a 'need to know' basis.

The ten committee men would each between them secretly tell one hundred of their countrymen the plan. Those one hundred would tell one thousand. Those one thousand would tell ten thousand. Those ten thousand would tell one hundred thousand, and so on until all the members in their Independence for India movement had been told. Goondhi had worked it out that everybody who needed to know would have been told within forty-eight hours. This was to become known as 'informed gossip'. There were ten million members in the movement. All would be told the plan in strictest confidence, with the threat of the monster of Katmandu being unleashed on anybody who broke it.

They each had to be simply told, 'VD Day November the first. If you whisper a word of this to anybody your throat will be torn out by the monster of Katmandu.' That was all. They each knew what they had to do.

It was planned that at 900 hours on the day of the cricket match, ten million Indians would leave their homes, each with just a teaspoonful of the strongest vindaloo curry ever concocted hidden upon their person. Even if the British rulers were to, as had been rumoured, introduce a stop-and-search policy they would hardly realise that the mountain of curry for which they had been searching was on the move. A teaspoonful at a time. This became known as a moveable feat.

There were five hundred thousand targets, each of which would get a delivery of twenty teaspoonfuls of a special curry cocktail that had been prepared with the strongest spices known to man. Just a grain would be enough to cause violent eruptions of the stomach.

The targets were all the army cookhouses, British government bases, homes of wealthy British businessmen and the city restaurants where the British civil servants ate their lunches and dinners.

In every kitchen, a sympathiser had been planted whose job it would be to mix the curry in with the dish of the day. Goondhi's non-violent movement was going to cause a violent movement of British bowels.

It had been calculated that by midday on November the second there would not be a single British soldier, government official or businessman who would be capable of standing. All would be forced to sit, helpless with their trousers and knickers down. While they were immobilised, the members of the Independence for India movement would take over all the British-run offices, dismantle all the weapons and war machinery, and systematically sabotage the civil service and British-dominated business networks by burning all records and making false orders.

Goondhi would then issue a warning that unless the British withdrew from India within seven days, a lethal dose of curry would be administered to each of them.

India would have its independence without a shot being fired, and the bottom would have been knocked out of the British Empire. Queen Victoria would no longer be the Empress on the throne, but all her subjects in India would be reluctant prisoners of the smallest throne.

Unaware of the double sting of the invasion threat from the Burpas and the approaching VD Day, Captain Ffortescue-Ffortescue put all his concentration on finding a winning cricket team for the Governor. He used his initiative and had all the mosquito nets that had been supplied when they left London for the Boer War sewn together and converted into cricket nets. It seemed a good idea at the time, but every insect in Kalabar seemed attracted to the netting and net practice had to be abandoned because everybody who ventured near them was swarmed over and bitten in any exposed fleshy part of the body. The Captain himself was an early victim, and his face was puffed up and positively glowing around his already bandaged nose. 'I have been butten to biggery,' he reported to the Sergeant-Major. 'You will have to take over the tricket crials.'

Sergeant-Major Thomas was a blood-and-guts, up-and-at-'em, up-and-under, hit-'em-between-the-posts rugby fanatic, who quite frankly considered cricket a poof's game. But he appreciated the importance of the match, and he did his best to organise a team. As he did not know the difference between a leg before, a leg break and a leg bye (even a leg over was but a distant memory), the Sergeant-Major was struggling.

The batsmen and bowlers playing for match day places in a trial game in the barracks square found it rather disconcerting having the Sergeant-Major, in his role as umpire, bellowing at the top of his voice after each six balls, 'Over the top!' When bowlers and fielders appealed with shouts of 'How's that?' he would answer, 'How's what?' It was also a little off-putting to the batsmen when he ran alongside them from wicket to wicket, thinking that he too was getting runs on the board. The true cricketers among the rabble decided to withdraw from the game when the Sergeant-Major started to demand that the batsmen stand to attention at the wicket, and that the fielders should march to and from their positions.

Some sanity was restored to this little corner of England that was a foreign field by the arrival from the officer's mess of Lieutenant Montague Grimcock. The suave, sophisticated Middlesex all-rounder, silk cravat around his neck and wearing a multi-coloured Old Etonian peaked cap, took charge of the game, relegating the Sergeant-Major to backward of deep mid-on which meant that he was fielding on the other side of the fort wall.

Within three hours, the Lieutenant had sorted the wheat from the chaff, and he reckoned there were six what he would call passable players including a big hitter from Birmingham named Arden, whom he would recommend for a County trial when they got back to Blighty. He was, unfortunately, a common player rather than a gentleman, but he could certainly thump a ball and had the Sergeant-Major dashing about among the

1. Bunghit Din (Bernard Bresslaw, left) joins forces with the Khasi of Kalabar (Kenneth Williams) against the British. *BFI Stills*

2. Sir Sidney Ruff-Diamond (Sidney James) gets a report from up the Khyber from Private James Widdle (Charles Hawtrey, left).

3. The Khasi of Kalabar (Kenneth Williams) has taken on more than he can handle in Lady Ruff-Diamond (Joan Sims). *BFI Stills*

4. Private Widdle (Charles Hawtrey), reappearing in the book as Mudyard Tipling, is bearded in the harem.

5. Captain Keene (Roy Castle, right) gets a pointed warning which is ignored by Sergeant-Major McNutt (Terry Scott). *BFI Stills*

7. Private Widdle (Charles Hawtrey, left) and Sergeant-Major McNutt (Terry Scott) are on the run as Queen Victoria's Barmy Army beat the retreat. *BFI Stills*

8. Brother Belcher (Peter Butterworth) is caught trying to convert a harem wife by Captain Keene (Roy Castle) and Sergeant-Major McNutt (Terry Scott). *BFI Stills*

10. (From left), Brother Belcher (Peter Butterworth), Sergeant-Major McNutt (Terry Scott), Private Widdle (Charles Hawtrey) and Captain Keene (Roy Castle) are ready to carry on in the harem. *BFI Stills*

11. Sir Sidney and Lady Ruff-Diamond (Joan Sims and Sidney James) and their house guests have just been caught by the Burpas. Not a pretty sight.

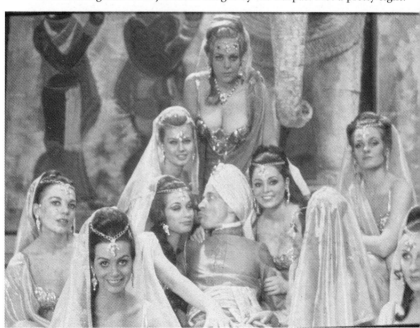

12. The Khasi of Kalabar (Kenneth Williams) and his harem delights.

cows and goats outside the fort retrieving the ball. Each time he managed to catch it he would shout 'Mark' and kick it back over the wall and loudly claim three points on the scoreboard.

A wee Scotsman from Glasgow called McKnacker was full of enthusiasm, and the Lieutenant felt the way he gave bowlers the charge with his bat held aloft like a claymore could give them a psychological advantage, psycho being the operative word.

Including himself, the Governor as Captain, the poet Mudyard Tipling, who described himself as a spinner of tails, and Captain Ffortescue-Ffortescue, Grimcock reckoned they had ten players who could play up, play up and play the game.

What they desperately lacked was a spinner, somebody who could make use of what were notoriously slow wickets in India. Grimcock was being fanned as he stood at the wicket in the middle of the parade ground wondering what to do about the missing link. 'Would the most honourable Lieutenant of the mighty army of Queen Victoria, God Bless her, like me to provide him with a service of balls while he gets his wonderful batting eye in?' asked Ginga Don.

The Lieutenant did not take kindly to being spoken to by a servant without first addressing him, but he decided to pay him for his effrontery by thrashing him all over the ground.

'All right, Sooty, you can bowl me a few balls,' he said, swishing his bat with imaginary wristy shots outside the leg and off stumps.

The first ball that Ginga Don bowled must have hit

97

a piece of loose gravel on the parade ground pitch, and the Lieutenant smiled as it removed his middle stump.

The second ball was a completely freak delivery that landed a full two yards outside the leg stump and knocked back the middle stump as the Lieutenant thrashed at thin air.

'For goodness sake try to give me a ball that I can hit,' he shouted irritably down the pitch at the ever grinning Ginga Don.

'I will pitch this ball right up for you, most estimable master of cricket,' said the double-jointed fanwallah.

The third ball was ballooned high towards the Lieutenant, Ginga Don's right arm seeming to bend like rubber at the moment of delivery. Grimcock advanced down the wicket and fired a perfect straight drive for six, at least it would have been perfect had he connected, but he was beaten by the flight and he heard behind him the death rattle of falling stumps.

By the time he had been beaten all ends up by the fourth and fifth balls, Grimcock realised he had found his spinner even though he was just a native and provided, of course, he did not enter the field of play from the same entrance as the gentlemen cricketers.

He had the satisfaction of getting his bat to the sixth ball, and sent it screaming at shoulder-height straight towards the fort wall. The bowler took off to his right like a high-flying bird and held a magnificent one handed catch.

'Okay, fanwallah,' said the Lieutenant. 'That will do for today. I've given you enough practice. Next time I will show you what batting is all about. Now then, how would you like to represent the Governor's team in the match against the Khasi's Eleven?'

Ginga Don threw himself prostrate at Grimcock's feet and started kissing them. 'Oh most worthy and noble master, you are saying the most wonderful words that have ever blessed my ever listening ears,' he said. 'How much must I pay you for this glorious distinction? You can have all the rupees I possess for me to have the chance to bowl against the Great Ranjitsinhji.'

'Get up you silly little man,' said an embarrassed Grimcock. 'You do not have to pay a fee, but don't get carried away with ridiculous notions that you will be playing against cricketers of the calibre of Ranjitsinhji. This is just the Khasi of Kalabar's local side.'

Ginga Don still had his turbaned head down by Grimcock's feet. 'A thousand thousand pardons, oh high and mighty one, but the Great Ranjitsinhji is *the* local hero. There would be much rioting and smashing of property if he were not to play as has been promised and, indeed, published in the esteemed, they-always-check-their-facts *Kalabar Chronicle*.'

Lieutenant Grimcock, who had been sent to join the 4th Foot and Mouth Regiment while he recovered from some mild shell-shocking at Ladysmith, suddenly felt his face distorting and his eyes blinking rapidly as had happened when the third grenade in as many minutes had exploded just feet from his trench.

Ranjitsinhji was one cricketer whose feet he would willingly kiss. He would have to tell the Governor that their task was hopeless, even with the hidden weapon of the rubbery-armed fanwallah.

The cricket trial over, everybody returned to the barracks. Sunlight had surrendered to the evening gloom and a jolly party was in progress in the officers' mess when Lieutenant Grimcock suddenly remembered that nobody had told the Sergeant-Major that the trial game had finished.

'Oh dash it,' he said, as he passed the port to Captain Ffortescue-Ffortescue. 'I forgot to tell that blasted loud-mouthed Sergeant-Major that the trial was over. He was fielding beyond the fort wall.'

'Hod sim,' said a very drunk Captain, who was hoping that sinking gallons of port would bring a darker shade of red to his cheeks to counter the glowing pinkness of the insect bites. 'It will do him good to do some fightime nielding. Lesh talk about more important thingsh. What was it like cooing it with that damel?'

Beyond the fort wall, Sergeant-Major Llandudo Thomas, never one to desert his post, was squinting up at the darkening sky on the look out for dropping cricket balls. He would have been much happier trying to catch oval-shaped balls.

It had been decided by the toss of a double-headed coin to play the match at the Khasi's private ground, which was a carefully manicured and regularly watered pitch set in the beautiful surroundings of the palace gardens.

The great Ranjitsinhji, soon to inherit his father's title as Maharajah, had arrived with his twelve bag-carriers and he smoothly and effortlessly struck fifty successive boundaries as a queue of the Khasi's servants lined up to bowl so that he could have batting practice on an

100

identical surface to the match pitch.

When the Khasi came on to bowl, he allowed him to hit his middle stump as a gesture of goodwill towards his host. The Khasi reacted in a rather ungentlemanly manner, running round the perimeter of the pitch with his fists punching the air, screaming, 'Gotcha!' It was a habit that he had picked up after buying a cricket blue at Oxford.

The great Ranjitsinhji was allowed to select the team, on the understanding that he invited the Khasi to be the Captain and to open the batting and the bowling. He picked nine other players from Kalabar who would all have been of international standard had the British authorities allowed Indians to play Test cricket (a privilege for which they had to wait another thirty-two years).

Her Ladyship watched all the preparations with growing excitement mixed with apprehension. She was now in two minds whether she wanted the Khasi or her husband to win. She had been thinking about the good times with the Governor, and realised that he must have loved her to make such efforts to win her back. The Khasi, she found, had become a little cold towards her of late, and she would see to it that he warmed up if he was lucky enough to win her in the cricket match.

Meantime, the humping and grunting ban had been lifted. The wives were allowed one day of leisure a week, but there was another storm on the horizon for the Khasi. Her Ladyship was about to introduce the wives to a custom she had picked up on a visit to New York. It was called, 'Shop until you drop'.

Mudyard Tipling
A self portrait

THE BURPAS ARE COMING

The Burpas are on the attack;
Quick, lock up your daughters.
The Burpas are on the attack;
Quick, lock up your 'quarters.
The Burpas are on the attack;
Quick, lock up your waters.
The Burpas are on the attack;
Quick, lock out the slaughterers.

Mudyard Tipling
British India, 1900

7

THE Governor's team were brought the ten miles from Fort Phucka to the Khasi's palace in some style, borne along on top of colourfully decorated elephants as the cricket match was turned into an excuse for a festival. Every one of the ten thousand invited guests was garlanded with flowers, and the six elephants, hooked trunk to tail, made their way slowly, heavily, yet somehow gracefully, along a petal-strewn path running between a long avenue of cypress trees. Marching behind the elephants in ceremonial uniform, with Sergeant-Major Thomas and two bagpipers proudly at their head, came the 4th Foot and Mouth Regiment, with just a dozen left behind to guard the fort. Even the ever-grinning Ginga Don had a jumbo seat, something he was used to in his youth when he served the Khasi as an elephant boy.

Captain Ffortescue-Ffortescue sat alongside the Governor on the lead elephant, and they both swayed in rhythm with the elephant's walk. This fluent motion did not help the equilibrium of the Governor, who had already sunk half a bottle of gin to try to steady his taut nerves.

As the lead elephant lowered itself to allow for disembarkation on the lawn beside the palace, Sir Sidney pitched slowly forward and landed face first in front of the welcoming committee led by the Khasi and the Great Ranjitsinhji. The Captain dismounted in more conventional style, and bent down to help the Governor to his feet. The Khasi and Ranjitsinhji thought Sir Sidney and the Captain were salaaming, and both of them dropped to their knees to reciprocate.

'May the best team win,' said the Great Ranjitsinjhi, who was famous for his impeccable sportsmanship.

'As long as it is my team,' added the Khasi, who was notorious for his appalling sportsmanship.

'The important thing is not winning but paking tart,' said Captain Ffortescue-Ffortescue, who was famous for never being understood.

'Where's the bar?' said the Governor, who was notorious for his drinking capacity.

The match trophy – Her Ladyship – made her entrance on a roses-swathed elephant. The wives in the harem followed on foot behind. All of them, including Her Ladyship, were protected from public gaze by large silk screens because they were in purdah, which meant they were not to be looked upon by strangers. There was really no need for her Ladyship to be covered up, but the Khasi insisted on it.

The Governor could just make out his wife's blue eyes over the top of her double-veil yashmak, and it reminded him of how she used to look at him teasingly from beneath the sheets. He instinctively blew her a kiss, to which she responded with a reverse victory sign. She had learned this, Sir Sidney recalled, from a young cigar-smoking lieutenant they met in Bangalore, who was also a war correspondent and would-be politician. He had told them about how a handful of banks were running the world, because never had so much been owed by so many to so few. Sir Sidney sighed when he

104

pondered on how much he and Her Ladyship had shared together, and now he was having to rely on winning a game of cricket to try to win her back. 'Drinkswallah,' he shouted from the pavilion verandah, 'fetch me a large gin and tonic, and go easy on the tonic.'

It was agreed by the two captains that each side would provide one umpire. Sergeant-Major Thomas was disappointed to be turned down, and as consolation he was given the role of official scorer. Then, when he pointed out that he would be giving three points for every run and another two points when the ball went 'over the sticks', it was decided it might be better if he concentrated on being the team trainer.

Brother Belcher, who had played a lot of cricket while at Cambridge University, was elected to stand as the umpire representing the Governor's team. The Khasi nominated his younger brother, Khasitwo.

The Sergeant-Major, taking his role as trainer perhaps a little too seriously, insisted on his entire squad running two laps of the cricket field and then following him through an explosive sequence of exercises. All this kept the spectators greatly amused, particularly the sight of the two bagpipers showing all they possessed every time they bent down. Sir Sidney was so exhausted by the sudden burst of exercise that he had to be carried out for the tossing up ceremony. Her Ladyship's request to do the tossing was turned down.

The Khasi was persuaded by the Great Ranjitsinhji that it would be unsporting to use the double-headed coin that had won him choice of venue, and it was the out-on-his-feet Governor who won the toss. On the advice of Lieutenant Grimcock, he elected to bat.

While all the pleasant preliminaries were going on at the cricket match, rebel leader Bunghit Din was preparing his mighty fifty thousand-strong army for the attack on Fort Phucka. There had been a minor mishap as they mustered ready to leave the Khyber Pass. A section of Burpa soldiers, not spotting any see-it-say-it names on each other, let off a salvo of shots and a thousand men had been wiped out before Bunghit Din was able to get the message through to them that they had their names only on their backs. He expected them to use their memories to recognise each other face to face. The incident underlined the tension in the air as the Burpas prepared to set out on one of the most important assignments in their five thousand year history.

Scouts had reported back to Bunghit Din that the Fort was all but deserted, with just a dozen guards left on duty. Everybody else was at the cricket match. Bunghit had put down a revolt that morning when his men had started arguing that they would prefer to watch the cricket than attack the Fort.

There was a motion to put it to a show of hands, but Bunghit Din was determined not to have his leadership undermined. He had personally executed the ringleaders, including three of his generals. In sporting deference to them he swung his sword through their necks with a copybook late cut stroke for which the Great Ranjitsinhji was famous throughout the cricket world. He then gave the order to move out for what he had codenamed Operation Phucka.

With so much nervous pressure around, it was understandable in the circumstances that the Burpa advance troops should have slight sense of direction problems and, anyway, their map-reading had never been one of their strongest points. They set off the wrong way up rather than down the Khyber Pass, and four thousand of them were ambushed and captured by Afghans as they strayed just slightly off course into Afghanistan. Bunghit Din was quickly able to fathom what had gone wrong, and immediately gave an 'about turn' order. This command did not travel right down the line, and there was an hour of unarmed combat, Burpa against Burpa, as half of them continued to advance towards Afghanistan into the other half who were following the 'about turn' command.

At least it gave Bunghit Din the satisfaction of knowing that all the hours of training in the skills of martial arts had turned his men into great fighting machines, and half of them lay either dead or nursing broken bodies before he was able to restore order to the ranks. He himself had been unable to resist joining in the man-to-man fighting, and he tied twenty tribesmen into knots by using the wrestling tricks he had learned when watching the Brown Bomber Body Bender of Bombay knitting his father into a human hoop. He then had great fun rolling the knotted warriors down the Khyber Pass before he remembered that this was not a day for sport. This was a day for invasion.

And so it was that Bunghit Din set off at the head of

107

twenty-two thousand Burpa tribesmen on the way to take Fort Phucka. The first victory in their entire history was, Bunghit Don knew, on the horizon. On this historic day, he felt quite unstoppable.

Meanwhile, the Great Curry Powder Plot was encountering unforeseen difficulties. The ear-to-ear launch had worked perfectly to start with. The ten privileged committee members had each whispered to ten movement members the codewords, 'VD Day. November the first. If you whisper a word of this to anybody your throat will be torn out by the monster of Katmandu.' One hundred code carriers were each then supposed to have whispered into the ears of ten fellow members the identical VD Day instruction. But each of them was so petrified by the thought of having their throats torn out that they dare not tell another soul, not even their fellow Independence for India supporters waiting for news of the Plot. If only Goondhi, when writing the code, had made it, 'If you whisper a word of this to anybody *who is not a member of our movement* your throat will be torn out, etc.' It was a point that would be taken on board for any future plots.

What the loose, ambiguous wording meant was that of the ten million movement members who should have received the code, nine million nine hundred and ninety nine thousand, nine hundred failed to get on line, which, statistically speaking, even Goondhi's most fervent supporters had to later admit was a pretty poor show.

While the quiet revolutionary Goondhi sat relaxed meditating in his bungalow with his trusted committee men in the belief that the message was being whispered across India, it had actually not got beyond the borders of Kalabar.

So on the morning of VD Day, while the first runs were being scored in the cricket match and Bunghit Din was leading the revolting Burpas on an audacious invasion of India, just twenty people set out with teaspoonfuls of the most potent curry powder ever concocted. And they were all aiming for Fort Phucka. Another twenty later headed for the Governor's residence. The other four hundred thousand, nine hundred and ninety-eight British-owned targets were left untouched.

The opening over in the cricket duel was bowled by the Khasi, who considered himself a leg spinner of mesmerising powers. All the sycophants surrounding him agreed that he was the greatest bowler since the famous Francis Drake, while in actual fact he could not bowl for toffee. Lieutenant Grimcock opened the batting for the Governor's XI, partnered by Second Lieutenant Scratchwell-Smith. The first ball reached Grimcock on the second bounce, and he effortlessly dispatched it over the long-off boundary for six. 'Go on my son,' came the shout from the pavilion amid the otherwise polite applause, which suggested that Sir Sidney Ruff-Diamond's breeding was not all that it was cracked up to be. 'Most unlucky, brother,' said umpire Khasitwo, who was under orders to be scrupulously fair with his decisions – unless, his brother had told him, a defeat looked possible.

109

Grimcock scored three fours and a single off the Khasi's next four balls, three of which had been so wide that he had to run after them to connect. Scratchwell-Smith swung at the final ball of the over and succeeded only in knocking it on to his pads. It was a clear case of bat pad, but the Khasi's shout of ''Owzat!' was so loud that it started a minor stampede among the elephants, who charged on to the field trumpeting through their trunks. Once the elephants had been herded back behind the pavilion and their great dollops of dung had been cleared from the pitch, umpire Khasitwo raised his finger, giving Scratchwell-Smith out leg-before wicket.

The Governor's XI 19 for one.

Her Ladyship applauded wildly behind her silk screen. Somebody was out and somebody else was in. What great fun. Why, she wondered, had she wasted so many years ignoring such an exciting game. And why, she wondered as she looked across at the familiar hunched figure of Sir Sidney in the pavilion, had she wasted so many months ignoring her husband. It was only now, seeing him in the flesh again, that she realised just how much she loved him, for all his faults. She would never be able to love the Khasi in the same way, for all his wealth and his skill at the humping and grunting. She suddenly knew that it was the Governor's team that she wanted to win the match, and she wished she knew whether the nineteen for one that showed on the scoreboard was good news or bad news for Sir Sidney.

Lieutenant Grimcock was joined at the wicket by Private Arden, who had been a batterer of bowlers in his days in the Birmingham club cricket league before a

110

pressing paternity case had persuaded him to join Her Majesty's army. He was encouraged as he walked out to the middle by chants from his Foot and Mouth regimental mates. 'Her Majesty Queen Victoria's Barmy Army,' they sang, while waving their Enfield rifles above their heads. From the pavilion came the lone voice of Ginga Don: 'God Bless her.'

With a series of punishing on-drives, the elegant Grimcock rattled up three boundaries off the second over bowled by medium pacer Bhagwat Bedsip. Her Ladyship watched him with particular interest when she was informed that he could really make his balls swing.

The Governor's XI 31 for one, all of the runs coming off the bat of Grimcock in just two eventful overs.

The first two balls of the Khasi's second over were reluctantly signalled as wides by umpire Khasitwo after Arden had failed to connect with either of them despite throwing himself full length to try to make contact. The Khasi made another of his loud appeals off the third delivery as the ball struck Arden's pads when he was standing in front of first slip trying to hit it. The Khasi brothers had a nose-to-nose argument after Khasitwo ruled that it was not leg-before, and he was sent off for showing dissent.

His place behind the stumps was taken by the Khasi's uncle, Khasiunkh, who had been boasting in the pavilion before a ball was bowled that he had put a million rupees on the Khasi's team to win at odds of two to one. As Khasiunkh was already known to be half a million rupees overdrawn at the bank, there was just a little concern among the Governor's supporters that

111

he might not have been exactly the most impartial man to select as an umpire.

Arden battered the Khasi's next ball for six, scattering the harem wives as it crashed through their silk screen. Veils were flying everywhere as they ran around like headless chickens, and Queen Victoria's Barmy Army danced around chanting. 'You've all gorn quiet over there,' they screamed in unison while making reverse V-signs in the direction of the ten thousand Indian spectators looking back at them as if they were quite mad. Then they shouted encouragement to Arden. 'There's only one Private Ardie, one Priv-ate Ar-die, only one Priv-ate Ar-ar-die.' This, thought the prophet Brother Belcher, standing at square leg, will never catch on.

The Brummie Basher tried a repeat shot off the next delivery but succeeded only in skying the ball to deep square leg where the Great Ranjitsinhji made a spectacular running catch. You would have thought the Khasi had bowled the Great Ranjitsinhji himself. He was carried shoulder high around the pitch by his team-mates, with umpire Khasiunhk leading the applause. As one, the ten thousand Indian spectators, chanted: 'You have all of you gone dreadfully quiet over there,' and then switching to, 'There is only one Khasi, one Kha-si, only one Kh-ah-si.'

Brother Belcher thought to himself that perhaps this might catch on after all.

The Governor's XI 39 for two, and not three overs completed yet.

Her Ladyship was standing on her chair, her yashmak

112

down around her neck, chanting with the Indians and then joining in the counter-chants from the British soldiers.

Next to join Lieutenant Grimcock in the middle was Sergeant Stoppitt, a solid defensive player who knew how to block the ball but without any back lift so that it rarely moved more than a few inches away from his bat. He was the regimental goalkeeper, and famous as a shot stopper. The problem was he thought he had only to stop the ball, not score with it.

Stoppitt let the remaining balls of Khasi's over drift harmlessly by to second slip, with umpire Khasiunhk ignoring that they should have been signalled as wides.

At the end of the over the Great Ranjitsinhji managed to persuade the Khasi that he had done more than his share of bowling, and that he should take a well deserved breather before the British players fathomed his devious spinning action.

For the next hour it became almost like a normal game of cricket, with Stoppitt blocking every ball that came near him and leaving the run making to the arrogant but gifted Grimcock. By the first break for drinks, the Governor's X1 were 93 for two off 21 overs with Grimcock on 85 not out and Stoppitt yet to score.

Her Ladyship joined in chants of, 'There's only one Lieutenant Grimcock, one Lieut-enant Grim-cock, only one Lieut-en-ant Grim-co-cock.' Sir Sidney blew her another kiss from his seat in the pavilion. Her Ladyship blew a kiss back, but then rather spoilt the blossoming romantic mood by shouting, 'You're going to get your blankety head kicked in... you're going to get your

113

blankety head kicked in.' She had become one of Her
Majesty Queen Victoria's Barmy Army.

Bunghit Din proudly rode ahead of his revolting Burpas
as they stepped foot in British India on the well-trodden
path to Fort Phucka. They had a mile to go when
Bunghit Din, sitting astride a piebald pony that sagged
under his weight, signalled for his troops to fan out.
Unfortunately his signal was misinterpreted by those
warriors right at the back. They took his outstretched
arms to mean they should start spraying bullets. Ten
thousand men fell dead or wounded in the following
twenty minutes of bloody mayhem before Bunghit Din
managed to get a ceasefire command through to his
trigger-happy troops. On a day like today, he thought,
it was understandable that they had itchy fingers.

The shooting was clearly heard by the dozen guards
at Fort Phucka, and they took it to be the firework
display that the Khasi had planned at the palace. They
carried on with their games of cards, ignoring the
chefwallah walking past them into the cook house with
a small packet of curry powder hidden under his coat.
He had collected the twenty spoonfuls of special
powder from the Independence for India members.
Within ten minutes, the chefwallah had stirred the
potent substance into the lamb stew that was planned
for that evening's dinner for the entire regiment.

Bunghit Din waved his fourteen thousand warriors
forward, and they quickly and quietly surrounded the
fort. The twelve guards were heavily engrossed in their
game of whist in which each of them was staking a

114

week's wages, and they were totally unaware of the attack that was, eventually, coming their way. There was another unfortunate delay in the offensive when the pony carrying the enormous Burpa leader suddenly splayed its legs, and Bunghit Din was sent flying head first on to the rocky terrain. He was knocked cold, and his generals decided they should wait for him to come round before they launched an all-out assault. It was a hold-up that was to prove disastrous.

The Khasi's XI made an important breakthrough in the first over after the drinks interval, during which Sergeant-Major Thomas went out with a bucket and sponge and insisted on mopping the two batsmen in the style of a rugby trainer.

Lieutenant Grimcock came down the wicket to the third ball of an over bowled by the Great Ranjitsinhji, who was first change bowler for England and Sussex. He failed to connect and it was touch and go whether Grimcock had made his ground as wicketkeeper Farokh Deesigner whipped off the bails. All eyes and appeals were aimed at square leg umpire Brother Belcher, who turned and made a sign of a rectangle towards the pavilion.

'What does that mean exactly, sir?' asked a puzzled Great Ranjitsinhji.

'It is something that will become commonplace in cricket,' explained Brother Belcher. 'I will now get a signal from a third umpire who will decide whether the batsman is out.'

In the pavilion, a sulking Khasitwo raised a reversed

middle finger in the direction of his brother. Umpire Belcher took this as a sign that the batsman was out, and he dramatically held up a finger and by force of habit made a sign of the cross. Lieutenant Grimcock's magnificent innings had finished on 87.

The Governor's XI 95 for three off 22 overs.

Private Jock McKnacker was next to the wicket, and he had insisted on wearing his kilt much to the amusement of the crowd. The Indian spectators joined in with the Barmy Army, chanting, 'Show us, show us what you've got, show us what you've got.' Her Ladyship was up on her chair conducting.

McKnacker, holding his crossed bat like a claymore, took an almighty swing at his first ball from the Great Ranjitsinhji. It was a curving delivery that took a vicious kick off the pitch. McKnacker's bat swished thin air and the ball thumped into his sporran. There was an audible sound of indrawn breath right around the ground in general and from McKnacker in particular as he sank slowly to the ground making a noise like punctured bagpipes.

Her Ladyship was offering to rub him better, but before she could move Sergeant-Major Thomas had gone dashing out with the bucket and sponge. 'Don't worry boyho,' said the Sergeant-Major. 'I is here to bring you relief. I've rubbed many privates in my time.'

As McKnacker lay on the ground to have, not to put too fine a point on it, his knackers massaged, he said, 'Dinna rub 'em, Sergeant-Major. *Count* 'em.'

He was fit to continue after five minutes, and to show he was sorry for the incident the sporting Ranjitsinhji bowled the final two balls of his over underarm and McKnacker gratefully whacked each of them to the boundary for successive fours.

With Sergeant 'Stonewall' Stoppitt holding up his end with a straight bat, the Governor's XI moved the score along during the next ten overs thanks to some ferocious hitting by McKnacker, who frightened the life out of the bowlers, and umpire Khasiunkh, by charging down the wicket to every ball. He was five runs short of his fifty when he was out in rather bizarre circumstances. A disguised back-of-the-hand Chinaman from spinner Vinoo Bhaggi brushed the underside of his bat and the ball became trapped in the hem of his kilt. He and Stoppitt raced up and down the pitch piling on the runs with the Indian fielders chasing after McKnacker. It was Bhaggi who finally got to him, lifting the ball from the hem and claiming a catch. The umpires consulted before Brother Belcher gave the dreaded sign of the cross, and they decided that seven of McKnacker's eight runs could count, so he departed to the pavilion with a very creditable 52 to his name. Many years later cricket historians searched through their *Wisden Almanacks*, but could not find anything to match the scorer's unique entry: McKnacker caught in the kilt by Bhaggi, 52.

The Governor's XI 147 for four off 32 overs. Stonewall Stoppitt was yet to get off the mark.

There was a long delay before the next batsman came in. This was Second Lieutenant Bendover, who was in charge of the regiment's ordnance unit. He got lost on the way to the wicket, turning left instead of right as he came down the pavilion steps. The dreadfully short-sighted Bendover was eventually found stumbling around among the elephants at the back of the pavilion, and was steered to the wicket where first of all he took his guard *behind* the stumps. He had to be persuaded that he could not stand at the same end as his batting partner Stoppitt, and was led to the correct set of stumps by Brother Belcher. Bendover survived just three balls before being run out after racing to square leg for a quick single. He returned to the pavilion thirty minutes later after wandering around the palace grounds, and, not for the first time, Sergeant-Major Thomas wondered if he was the ideal person to be in charge of the regiment's ordnance surveys.

The Governor's XI 147 for five off 32 overs.

Her Ladyship believed she was now getting the hang of the game, and was keeping the harem wives informed of the progress. 'My husband's team are one hundred and forty-seven wickets for five runs against your husband's team,' she said, repeating it forty-seven times so that she was not seen to be favouring any of the wives.

Meanwhile, back at the Fort, there was something of a catastrophe for the revolting Burpas. The generals regretted their decision not to go ahead without their leader because when Bunghit Din came round his brains were scrambled. 'Shoot on sight!' he roared. 'Take no prisoners.' If he had been thinking straight he knew better than anybody that the one order you never ever gave to a Burpa was shoot on sight because they took it quite literally. They started shooting everything in

118

sight, and as the only targets they could see were fellow warriors this order from Bunghit Din was, to put it mildly, pretty cataclysmic for the Burpas.

Inside the Fort, the dozen card-playing guards peeped out through the wall spyholes and said in unison, 'Sod this for a game of soldiers.' They escaped through an underground tunnel along with the chefwallahs and the stable staff. The Fort was now deserted.

The historic Battle of Fort Phucka lasted just fifty-five minutes during which thirteen thousand three hundred Burpas were wiped out.

Bunghit Din led the seven hundred survivors into the Fort with tears welling in his eyes. As they entered the Fort in triumph, marching with their chests puffed out, they proudly whistled their army song, 'Colonel Ramsinghbogey'.

It was Bunghit Din who personally pulled down the Union Jack and ran the Burpa flag up the poll. It was the greatest day in the long history of the Burpas.

He had achieved the first of his three objectives. Next was the kidnapping of Her Ladyship, and then the plundering of the treasure. But first the victorious army sat down to a banquet fit for a king, with delicious lamb stew as the main course.

Captain Ffortescue-Ffortescue, oblivious to what was going on back at the Fort, was seventh man in for the Governor's XI. It took several minutes before he could receive his first ball because of a communications problem with umpire Khasiunkh. Asking for his guard, the Captain said: 'Liddle and meg, please.'

Khasiunkh scratched his head. 'What is this liddle and meg?' he asked the Great Ranjitsinhji, who was equally perplexed.

'I have played the wonderful game of cricket all around the world,' he said, 'but this I have never heard of.'

Sergeant-Major Thomas, bucket and sponge in hand, came racing out to the middle. 'I think what the Captain means, begging your pardon for sticking my nose in, Captain,' said the Sergeant-Major, 'is middle and leg.'

'That's what I sust jaid,' said the Captain. 'Give me liddle and meg and let's get on gith the wame.'

Umpire Khasiunkh shrugged, and gave the Captain middle-and-leg for his guard mark. During the next ten overs, the Captain managed to scramble ten runs against some tight bowling. He then aggressively hooked Bedsip for a four, and the Barmy Army came back to life. 'There's only one Captain Ffortescue-Ffortescue, one Captain Ffortescue-Ffortescue, only one Cap-tain Ffort-es-cue-Ffort-es-cue,' they sang with some difficulty. By the time they had finished the chant, the Captain was back in the pavilion.

He tried a repeat shot off the next ball and ballooned it for what should have been a comfortable catch to the Khasi at first slip. He fumbled the ball which was dropping to the ground when the Great Ranjitsinhji dived full length and pushed it back up for the Khasi to make the catch. The ten thousand invited guests in the crowd, all of them either related to the Khasi or in his debt, rose as one, borrowing a Barmy Army chant: 'Ooh, aah, Khasi-ah... ooh, aah, superstar...'

You could have cut the tension out in the middle of

120

the playing field with a knife, and the Khasi was his usual sporting self as he pointed Ffortescue-Ffortescue towards the pavilion with the send off, 'On your bike, pal,' which was another bad habit he had picked up in the Parks at Oxford.

'There's no need for that sort of lile vanguage,' said the Captain. 'Just lutton your bip.'

Brother Belcher stepped between them. 'Gentlemen, gentlemen,' he said. 'This is only a game. Mind you, the time will come when an England Captain will come to this continent and prod an umpire with his finger. At least you have not yet sunk to that level.'

The Khasi prodded Belcher in the chest. 'Just shut it, ump,' he said. 'I would not lift a finger to help you.'

The Great Ranjitsinhji, acknowledged throughout cricket as the first gentlemen of the sport, was the only man big enough and courageous enough to be able to give the Khasi a ticking off over his behaviour. 'Let us beat them with a smile rather than a snarl, my friend,' he said. 'I will personally see to it that you win the fair hand of the maiden.'

Khasi looked to the wives' section alongside the pavilion and saw that Her Ladyship was teaching his wives how to chant. 'We're the Khasi's Barmy Army,' they sang like a heavenly choir. 'Nobody likes us, we don't care.'

He looked forward to personally executing 'the fair maiden' when the game was won. He would take great delight in making it 'maiden over'.

The Governor's XI 161 for six off 42 overs. Stonewall Stoppitt was still unbeaten on nought.

121

Mudyard Tipling was next to the crease, and to inspire himself he walked to the middle reciting Henry Newbold's *Vita Lampada*, wishing that it was one of his compositions...

'There's a breathless hush in the close tonight;
Ten to make and the match to win.
A bumping pitch and a blinding light,
An hour to play and the last man in.
And it's not for the sake of a ribboned coat,
Or the selfish hope of a season's fame,
But his Captain's hand on his shoulder smote:
"Play up! Play up! and play the game!".'

One minute later Mudyard was walking back to the pavilion. He played up, in fact too uppishly, and presented an easy caught-and-bowled chance to the Great Ranjitsinhji off the first ball that he received. As he disconsolately returned to where he had come, Mudyard composed a mood poem of his own that captured just what he thought of the moment, and which he sang to himself in the calypso style that he had learned while once on a mission to the West Indies:

'Cricket, lousy cricket, what a great shame
I've lost my wicket;
Cricket, lousy cricket, no run to my name
And I can't stick it;
Play down, play down, can't play the game.'

Her Ladyship was standing up on her chair cheering as

Mudyard walked back without having troubled the scorer. 'That is a very clever man,' she informed the harem wives. 'He has just laid a duck's egg.'

The wives were most impressed, and responded with an impromptu chorus of, 'Ooh-aah, Mudyard-ah... ooh-ahh, superstar...'

Mudyard was moved to tears by this, while the Khasi glared from first slip. He was allowed to be the only superstar in their lives. Another black mark against Her Ladyship. He would use the one thousand cut execution technique.

The Governor's XI 161 for seven off 42 overs. Stonewall Stoppitt was still unbeaten on nought.

The eighth man in was Lance Corporal Sean 'Paddy' O'Shaughnessy, who had impressed Lieutenant Grimcock in the trial match with his throwing arm. It was a technique he had perfected while playing semi-professional baseball when staying with relatives in Boston.

He stood waiting for his first delivery with his cricket bat crossed and held at shoulder height. Ranjitsinhji was so astonished that he bowled a rare loose ball, and O'Shaughnessy swung and connected with a shot that sent the ball sailing over the heads of the crowd into the artificial lake beyond the pavilion. The umpires and fielders, not forgetting Stonewall Stoppitt, were just a little disconcerted when the Irishman dropped his bat and raced around the field before skidding to a stop back at the wicket. As far as he was concerned he had scored a home run, and he was amazed to find himself credited with six runs on the scoreboard.

The Foot and Mouth supporters were ecstatic. 'O'Shaughnessy,' they sang, 'we're proud to sing that name... while we sing this song we'll win the game.'

Her Ladyship and the wives were much more inventive. 'Knick knack Paddy whack, give the ball a crack,' they chanted, while the Khasi quietly considered two thousand cuts.

The lead chanter with the Foot and Mouth supporters became quite ambitious.

'Give me an O,' he shouted, 'Give me an S... give me an H... give me an....'

He then realised he could not spell the surname, and settled for spelling out the name Paddy, with his mates shouting each letter after him.

Stoppitt had a quiet word with O'Shaughnessy and explained to him the fundamentals of running between rather than round the wickets.

'You mean oi can be taking a short cut?' the Irishman said. 'Now oi wonder why dey're never taught of dat in baseball. It would save an awful lot of energy if dey were to run straight, so it would.'

'But that wouldn't be cricket, old boy,' said Stoppitt, which brought a rapid conclusion to that particular conversation.

O'Shaughnessy survived the next two deliveries after lashing out wildly and missing the ball by inches. He was convinced that if he missed the next ball he would be struck out as in baseball, and when he managed to make a connection he dropped his bat and raced off to his right by force of habit. Stoppitt jogged a single to the non-striker's end and then concentrated on shouting the Irishman home. 'Left, left, Paddy,' he shouted. 'Back ten yards this way. Stay there!'

He had got him back to base before the bails were removed. At the end of the over, Stoppitt summoned O'Shaughnessy to the middle for a tactical talk.

'Now listen, Paddy,' he said, 'I'm going to concentrate on keeping my end up.'

'And what will oi be doing while you're having all the fun?' asked Paddy.

'You just have a swinging time with your bat,' said Stoppitt. 'But don't keep dropping it. You run with it in your hand and straight up and down the pitch.'

'Dat's a handicap system dey've not taught of in baseball,' he said. 'Running wid the bat. I shall wroite to my cousins in Boston and suggest it, so I shall.'

Stoppitt looked at Vinoo Bhaggi taking the ball for the next over. 'Now they're bringing their crafty spinner back on,' he warned. 'Watch out for his back-of-the-hand googlies.'

'Now dere's a ting,' said Paddy. 'Oi've heard of all koinds of tings, but never googlies coming out of the back of the hand. He would make a fortune as a pitcher in America, so he would.'

Vinoo tied O'Shaughnessy into all sorts of knots with his first three deliveries. After his third successive miss, the Irishman walked slowly back towards the pavilion with his head down in disappointment. He had to be persuaded by square leg umpire Brother Belcher that his innings was not over.

'You're only dismissed if the ball hits your stumps, your pads in front of the wicket, you're caught by a fielder or you are run out,' he explained.

'Begorrah,' said an astonished Paddy, 'you mean I can miss the ball more dan tree toimes and still bat on? Just wait until my cousins in Boston hear about dis. Dey don't give you enough chances to hit the ball out there, so dey don't.'

He watched Vinoo rubbing the ball up and down his thigh as he tried to keep the shine on it for the swing bowlers. 'Now whoi is everybody having fun out here except me?' he said. 'Would you look at what dat man's doing with his googlies. And in full sight of all the Khasi's woives. Oi've never seen anything loike it in my loife, so oi haven't.'

Similar thoughts were going through the mind of Her Ladyship as she watched the ball-rubbing process. She considered it one of the most erotic things she had ever seen, and she silently vowed never to miss another cricket match as long as she lived. She got particularly aroused when told that Vinoo was notorious for tampering with his balls, and picking the stitches so that they would perform better. She did not realise that balls had stitches, and decided that she would make a closer inspection at the first opportunity.

The next unstitched ball from Vinoo hit the shoulder of O'Shaughnessy's bat and went straight up in the air. As the ball came down, Paddy caught it.

There were roared appeals, and umpire Khasiunkh signalled that he was out.

'You said oi was only out if a fielder caught the ball,' Paddy moaned to Brother Belcher on his way back to the pavilion.

'Well you found a new way out,' he replied. 'It's called obstructing the field.'

'But oi didn't do anything to the field,' said Paddy. 'All oi did was catch the ball. Dis cricket will never catch on. It's too complicated. Dey should keep it simple loike in baseball, so they should.'

The Governor's XI 168 for eight off 44 overs. Stonewall Stoppitt was still unbeaten on nought.

There were good-natured jeers when Ginga Don next came to the wicket, moving up one in the order while they tried to sober up the Governor with a cold shower. Ginga Don was considered something of a turncoat playing for the Governor's team, but as he had carried out listening duties for virtually everybody in the crowd they wanted to see him succeed, provided, of course, he did not prove a match winner.

Ginga Don fanned the wicket keeper while he was waiting for his first delivery, which he neatly turned away for a four down at the fine leg boundary.

The Barmy Army were back in full voice. 'Ginga, Ginga, Ginga Don,' they chanted imaginatively, 'Ginga, Ginga Don.'

Proving himself nearly as good a batsman as he was a bowler, Ginga Don quickly added another forty runs to the total before the Great Ranjitsinhji came back on to bowl.

The overawed fanwallah was so busy salaaming to his hero that he made no attempt to hit the ball that removed his middle stump. 'A thousand thank yous for removing my stump, oh world's most wonderful master of cricket,' Ginga Don said, overjoyed to have been the victim of the Great Ranjitsinhji.

The Governor's XI, including extras, 212 for nine off 48 overs. Stonewall Stoppitt was still unbeaten on nought.

A buzz went round the ground as the Governor came out to bat, escorted – or, rather, supported – by Lieutenant Grimcock. It had been agreed that he could act as a runner for Sir Sidney, who was said to have a slight fever which was causing him to stagger. The fact that he had poured a bottle of gin down his throat since the match started was not mentioned.

At the sight of his sworn rival coming from the pavilion, the Khasi started to perform leg stretching warm-up exercises and rotated his arms ready to be recalled to the attack.

Of the three balls coming towards him at once from the Great Ranjitsinhji, the cross-eyed Governor amazingly selected the right one to hit and he survived four deliveries before pushing the final ball of the over down the wicket. Stoppitt decided there was a single and called 'one'. Sir Sidney forgot that he had a runner and started to scamper down the wicket, with Grimcock running beside him. The Great Ranjitsinhji raced to field off his own bowling, and got tangled up with the Lieutenant. 'Out of the bloody way, Sooty,' he shouted.

Sir Sidney made his ground, although his official runner was way short. The umpires conferred, and were about to give Sir Sidney out when the Great Ranjitsinhji persuaded them that it should count as a run because he had accidentally obstructed the runner. He was too much of a gentleman to comment on Grimcock's offensive 'Sooty' remark, but he silently vowed to make him pay for it.

As the ball was tossed to the Khasi, a sudden hush fell on the ground. It had all the tension and drama of a high noon duel as Sir Sidney prepared to face his first delivery.

The Khasi took a sixty yard run up, which was rather unusual for a man who specialised in slow wrist spinners. He released the ball two yards before the crease and it smashed into the back of the head of umpire Khasiunkh. Fortunately for him he was wearing the caps and hats of all the fielders balanced on his turban, and he was only slightly concussed. He first of all raised a finger to signal that Sir Sidney was out, but was persuaded by the Great Ranjitsinhji that the correct decision was a dead ball.

The Khasi was exhausted after his sixty yard gallop, and elected to bowl his next ball off a three step run. The ball looped towards the Governor, who closed his eyes and swung. There was a roar from the Foot and Mouth supporters as the ball soared away to the pavilion for a six.

'There's only one Governor Ruff-Diamond,' they chanted, 'one Governor Ruff-Diamond... one Gov-er-nor Ru-ff-Dia-mond.'

Her Ladyship was leaping up and down in excitement. 'Go on Sidney,' she shouted. 'Give it to him. Right up the Khyber.'

The harem wives chorused, 'Right up the Kh-yb-er.'

As he turned for his next delivery, the Khasi's mind was on five thousand cuts. His loose long-hop was heading for the slips, and Sir Sidney took a swing at it. He lost the grip on his bat, which flew down the pitch like a javelin and thumped umpire Khasiunkh high on the head. Once again, he was saved from serious damage by his turban and the fielders' hats. The Governor had the good grace to apologise. 'I'm shorry, Khashiunkh,' he slurred. 'The bat shlipped out of my hand.'

The dazed umpire responded by raising a finger, and while the Khasi was running around celebrating a wicket the Great Ranjitsinhji once again had to tell him that the Governor was not out.

The Khasi's next ball reached the Governor on the third bounce, and as it rolled past him he went down on his knees to take a swipe at it and succeeded only in knocking all of his three stumps out of the ground.

There was pandemonium in the ground as the Khasi raced down the pitch with his arms raised aloft. 'Take some of that!' he yelled into the Governor's face before he was grabbed by spectators who had come racing from their seats. They carried him in triumph back to the pavilion.

'It'sh not all over yet,' shouted Sir Sidney as he was helped back to the pavilion by Lieutenant Grimcock and Stonewall Stoppitt, who had surely created some sort of record by finishing nought not out after facing one hundred and seventeen deliveries. He later explained in an interview with the man from the *Kalabar Chronicle* that he had learned his defensive technique from watching Woolwich Arsenal play football. 'You must never ever be adventurous,' he explained, 'and keep your posts covered at all times.'

The Governor's XI 219 all out, Stonewall Stoppitt unbeaten on nought.

Watching the Khasi being carried off by jubilant supporters, Her Ladyship thought the match must be all over and she burst into tears. This, she thought, meant the end of her marriage to Sir Sidney. But she brightened when it was explained that now that the Governor's team was out, the Khasi's team would go in and that Sir Sidney's team would be out in the field. 'Ah,' she nodded knowingly. 'In and out, in and out. This will appeal to Sidney.'

She turned to the harem wives. 'It's not over yet,' she told them, 'My Sidney's still got a lot of balls to play with.'

The harem wives were most impressed.

Her Ladyship waved in encouragement to Queen Victoria's Barmy Army. They responded with a chant of, 'One Lady Ruff-Diamond, there's only one Lady Ruff-Diamond, one La-dy Ru-ff-Di-am-ond.'

The harem wives joined in the second chorus, and looking on from the pavilion the Khasi wondered if he could get into the *Genius Book of Records* with ten thousand execution cuts.

Mudyard Tipling
A self portrait

A STICKY WICKET

The runs, they are being run
The wickets, they are falling,
It's cricket in the sun
And it's all quite appalling.
The Khasi's playing up
Because he cannot win.
Her Ladyship is the cup;
He'd rather a kicked shin.

Mudyard Tipling
British India, 1900

132

8

SERGEANT-Major Thomas was just about to attack a whole fresh lobster during the tea interval between the two innings when he felt convinced he spotted one of the Fort guards chanting along with 'Her Majesty Queen Victoria's Barmy Army'. He ordered Private Arden to keep an eye on his lobster – 'don't let hanybody nick a single claw,' he said – and then walked across the cricket field to where the Foot and Mouth soldiers were making heavy inroads into the dozens of crates of English beer that they had brought with them from the barracks.

Sure enough, his razor-sharp eyesight had not been deceiving him. 'Private Tompkins,' he roared, 'who's holding the Fort?'

Tompkins broke off in mid-chorus on a rendering of 'The Old Bull and Bush', and blanched as he looked back at the Sergeant-Major, an intimidating figure even though he was wearing a large bib ready for his assault on the lobster.

'The Burpas are, Sir,' said Tompkins.

The Sergeant-Major could not believe what he was hearing. 'Say that again, boyho,' he said, now straining with every sinew to make sure he heard exactly what was being said above 'The Old Bull and Bush' chorus from the Barmy Army.

'The Burpas, Sir, they are holding the Fort, Sir,' said a terrified Tompkins.

The Sergeant-Major's face had turned the colour of

his yet to be devoured lobster, and his eyes were bulging so much that he looked ready to explode.

'What the hell d'you mean the Burpas is holding the Fort?' he roared.

'We did try to report it to Captain Ffortescue-Ffortescue, Sir,' said Tompkins, 'but it was just after he was out, and he told us to leave him alone until after the match was over.'

'Follow me, Private,' screamed a nearly apoplectic Sergeant-Major. 'Quick march, boyho. Left-right-left-right-left-right.'

They moved back across the cricket field to the pavilion at the double double, the boots of Private Tompkins barely touching the ground.

Captain Ffortescue-Ffortescue was winning the fight with his lobster, and was just about to crack open the second claw when the Sergeant-Major stamped to attention in front of him with a petrified-looking Private alongside him.

'Please leave me alone while I'm linishing my fobster,' said the Captain. 'And as for you, Private, I've already told you not to mother me until the batch is over.'

'Begging your pardon, Sir,' said the breathless Sergeant-Major, 'but this is a matter of hutmost hurgency.'

'You're not still sulking because we didn't let you umpire, are you Margeant-Sajor?' said the Captain, as he snapped open the lobster claw.

The Sergeant-Major bristled, his military moustache dancing up and down with indignation. 'Just tell the Captain what you has told me,' he ordered Private

Tompkins, who would rather have been making eyes down at The Old Bull and Bush.

'We did try to report to Captain Ffortescue-Ffortescue, but it was just after he was out...'

'Not that bit, you hidiot,' roared the Sergeant-Major. 'Tell him about who's holding the Fort.'

'The Burpas are holding the Fort, Sir,' said a quaking Tompkins.

The Captain dropped his lobster claw. 'I bon't delieve it!' he exclaimed. 'Are you telling me that the bamned Durpas have taken over Phort Fuckha?'

'Yes, Sir,' said Tompkins, now relating the story that he and his eleven fellow-guards had agreed on during their ten-mile walk to the cricket ground. 'They over-ran us after a bitter battle. We managed to wipe out most of them, but several hundred forced their way through the Fort gates and so we escaped under heavy fire.'

'How many do you think you managed to knock out?' asked the Sergeant-Major.

'At a rough guess, I would say twelve thousand,' said Tompkins.

'Thelve twousand,' said the Captain. 'Lad, gad, that's Crictoria Voss stuff. I'll see to it that you're dentioned in misdatches. Might met a gedal myself.'

'I'll muster the troops ready to march on the Fort,' said the Sergeant-Major, making a mental note to carry out a thorough investigation of the Tompkins report. It was something of a mystery to him how twelve guards could wipe out twelve thousand Burpas when there were only ten thousand bullets in the armoury.

'Horse your holds,' said the Captain. 'Let me report

this to the Governor and see what he binks is thest.'

The Governor, his judgement rather clouded by the quantity of gin he had consumed, decided that all efforts to recapture the Fort should be postponed until after the match. 'Lisshen,' he said, 'it would caushe an internashional inshident if we were to pull out of this game now. It would be shuggeshted that we are frightened of loshing.'

'I pake your toint,' said the Captain. 'But don't you think we could spare everybody except those taking mart in the tatch?'

'Shertainly not,' said Sir Sidney. 'The shupport of the sholdiers here is vital to ush. We need them cheering ush on if we're to beat the bloody Khashi.'

'Ses, yir, a dise wecision, if I may so say,' said the Captain.

'You can't shay any bloody thing,' snapped the Governor, who was letting the tension of the match get to him.

The Captain smartly saluted and then returned to his lobster. The Burpas could wait until the lobster was finished and the match was won.

Sergeant-Major Thomas could not wait to get to grips again with Bunghit Din. He had still not forgotten their face-to-face confrontation in the Khyber Pass cave when the monster had made a timely flaming appearance. It amazed him that they were not returning straight away to win back the Fort. How, he wondered, could they put a cricket match, of all things, first? Now if it had been a game of rugby, that would have been quite a different matter.

136

He returned to where he had left his lobster to find the wreckage of two empty claws. 'Sorry Sergeant-Major,' said a hugely satisfied Private Arden. 'Thought you'd gone to join the Barmy Army.'

Sergeant-Major Thomas tore off his bib, and dropped into a deep sulk.

While it was lobster on the menu at the cricket ground, it was lamb stew that was filling the empty stomachs of the triumphant Burpa warriors at Fort Phucka. 'It is,' said Bunghit Din, 'quite the finest stew I have ever eaten. This is what they must mean by the sweet taste of victory.' He had never known it before.

It was agreed that the strong curry flavour gave it a certain unique piquancy. 'Perhaps a little too tart for my personal taste,' said Bunghit Din, 'but buggers can't be choosers.'

He stood and addressed his troops after a dessert of figs and prune juice. 'This feast, my brave warriors,' he said, referring to notes he had scribbled on the back of the menu card, 'is just the start of the good life. We have had some wonderfully proud and immensely memorable days in our history. There was, for instance, that afternoon we had the Kashunkaries on the run until we were unfortunate enough to wander into our own minefield. These things happen in war. Then there was the day we forced the Kashunuts back twenty miles only for our mustard gas to blow back in our faces. These things happen in war. But this, today, is our finest hour.'

He paused and let that phrase drift around the banqueting room. Our finest hour. History will pick up on that one, he thought. Like all great statesmen, he knew how to capture a mood with a simple sentence.

'We have written a glorious new page in our history books,' he continued, 'and we have laid the foundation for a great future. Now we must prepare ourselves for a counter attack from the cowardly fiends who deserted this Fort today under our unstoppable advance. I will be going off on a lone mission for a few hours to get a certain insurance for us. While I am away I want you to set up defensive positions and a round-the-clock watch. I see us building a state of Burpaskhan, with Kalabar as our starting point. Today Kalabar, tomorrow the world.'

As he sat down to resounding cheers the warriors followed an old Burpa tradition of throwing everything left on the meal table. Unfortunately, the dinner knives – which they were not accustomed to using – had not been cleared, and another two hundred tribesmen had their lives needlessly wasted as knives, spoons and forks were hurled about with wild abandon.

It put a bit of a dampener on the day as far as Bunghit Din was concerned, and he was not in the best of spirits as he rode away from the Fort on Captain Ffortescue-Ffortescue's white charger.

The Khasi and the Great Ranjitsinhji came out to bat to rapturous applause from the invited spectators. During the tea interval the harem wives had knitted a huge banner that should have read, KNOCK THEM FOR SIX KHASI. It was the dyslexic wife who was in charge of the six, and the banner actually read, KNOCK THEM FOR SEX KHASI.

Her Ladyship had loudly cheered her husband's team

138

when they came out to field, but applauded only politely when the Khasi came out to bat. She now had no doubts about which team she wanted to win. There was something about the way the Khasi kept looking at her that sent shivers down her spine. Why, it was almost as if he hated her. Sir Sidney, on the other hand, had been looking at her through eyes that she was convinced were glazed with love. In actual fact he was drunk out of his head.

Lieutenant Grimcock took the new ball and prepared to bowl the first over, with the Khasi on the receiving end. He made a great fuss of taking his guard from Umpire Khasiunkh, who took a ruler down the wicket to make sure his bat was placed exactly at middle-and-off. Stonewall Stoppitt was the wicket-keeper, with the Governor half asleep at first slip alongside Captain Ffortescue-Ffortescue.

Grimcock, who bowled medium fast, had set an attacking field for his first delivery that he hurled down off a twenty-yard run. The ball whipped through the Khasi's defence and uprooted his middle stump. The fielders were just running to congratulate Grimcock on this instant breakthrough when there was a rather late call of 'no ball' from umpire Khasiunkh.

The second delivery beat the Khasi all ends up but lifted just over the top of the stumps. It was swinging away to the right and Stoppitt made a diving goalkeeper style save, and then amazed everybody by kicking the ball way down the pitch over the head of a startled Grimcock. The batsmen scrambled through for a single.

The Great Ranjitsinhji, remembering Grimcock's

'Sooty' insult, proceeded to punish him in the way he knew best. He smoothly guided the remaining five balls of the over away to the boundary for fours, and then doffed his cap to the ashen-faced lieutenant.

Everybody in the ground, with the exception of the silenced Barmy Army, joined in the chant of, 'There's only one Great Ranjitsinhji, there's only one Great Ranjitsinhji, one Gr-ea-t Ran-jit-sin-hji.' Even, Ginga Don, fielding at fine leg, sang along.

The Khasi's XI 22 for no wicket, Ranjitsinhji 20.

Sean O'Shaughnessy, who insisted on wearing his baseball glove, opened the bowling from the opposite end. He took no run up at all, and stood in a pitcher's stance with one leg raised before suddenly hurling a beamer towards the Khasi's head. The ball bounced off his turban, and the batsmen crossed for a bye. The Indian spectators booed and jeered, and the Barmy Army cheered. Her Ladyship picked up the quaint-sounding Barmy Army chant of, 'We're the head bangers of Kalabar... nobody likes us, we don't care.'

The Khasi looked the eighty yards to where Her Ladyship was swaying around with her arms in the air chanting, and gave quiet consideration to death by fifteen thousand execution cuts.

Brother Belcher warned O'Shaughnessy. 'That sort of bowling will cause an international dispute one day,' he said. 'If you persist in bowling bodyline* I will have no

---

*England's Test team were involved in a row with the Australians after being accused of bodyline tactics in the Ashes tour of 1932-33. The allegation was that the England bowlers, particularly Harold Larwood, were bowling at the man rather than the wicket. The intimidating tactics were the brainchild of England's Indian-born skipper Douglas Jardine.

alternative but to request that your skipper takes you off.'

'Takes me off where?' asked the Irishman, who was wearing his baseball cap back to front. 'Oi'm not going any place until oi've stopped these batters hitting so many home runs. Oi was a great success back in the Boston league with dis styoile, so I was. Oi don't bowl, oi pitch.'

His second ball, or as he more accurately described it, pitch, took the same trajectory. The Great Ranjitsinhji moved gracefully across to his leg stump and hooked the ball away to the mid-wicket boundary for a spectacular six. The following four deliveries were treated in similar contemptuous fashion, with two sixes and two fours. The crowd were in a frenzy of excitement, and just kept up a continual roar. The Barmy Army concentrated on drinking their beer.

'They don't like it up 'em,' it was suggested to Her Ladyship. 'Maybe not,' she said, 'but I do.'

The Khasi's XI 49 for no wicket, Ranjitsinhji 46 not out and three extras.

Shell-shocked Lieutenant Grimcock retired with broken pride after his one-over hammering by the Great Ranjitsinhji, who had paid him back for that Sooty remark in spades. Private Arden came on to bowl with his medium-pace cutters that had brought him fair success in the Birmingham league. His first ball rapped the Khasi on the glove, and he raced through for a quick single shaking his hand vigorously.

Her Ladyship was disgusted that he should make such rude gestures in public, but most of the other

141

people in the ground celebrated his first registered run as if it was the match-winning blow. Umpire Khasiunkh carried him around the pitch, and he waved his bat to all four sides of the ground. The sporting response from the Barmy Army was, 'You're going to get your blankety head kicked in.'

The Great Ranjitsinhji then gave Arden the treatment, sweeping him for two fours, driving him for a straight six and then running three off the final ball of his over after which the Brummie waved a white handkerchief in mock surrender.

Sergeant-Major Thomas thought he was summoning him, and he came dashing out with his bucket and sponge. To the amusement of the crowd, Arden sponged down the ball. 'The ball needs urgent treatment,' he said. 'It's being murdered.'

The Khasi complained that this constituted ball-tampering. Umpire Khasiunkh had no doubt whatsoever that his intelligent, influential and extremely rich nephew was correct, and a new ball was provided.

When her Ladyship heard that one of the players was tampering with his ball, she encouraged the forty-seven wives to break their purdah but they preferred to take her word for it. They dare not look.

The Khasi's XI 67 for no wicket, Ranjitsinhji 63 not out and three extras.

The new ball was quickly looking even more battered than the previous one as the Great Ranjitsinhji rocketed to an undefeated century in just forty-one minutes, with the Khasi stuck on one and rarely having to face a single ball because of the way he was being protected from

142

the bowling by his partner. Even the Barmy Army somewhat reluctantly joined in the applause for the Great Ranjitsinhji's century. Ginga Don, fielding on the boundary, was doing cartwheels in his excitement.

The Khasi's XI 112 for nought, Ranjitsinhji 101 not out and ten extras.

Everybody had a bowl in a bid to stop the onslaught, including the sozzled Governor who fell into the stumps as he delivered his first ball. He went for the maximum thirty-six runs off his one over as the Great Ranjitsinhji smashed a record six successive sixes. Umpire Belcher joined in the applause. 'This will be equalled one day in the distant future by somebody who is not sober,' he prophesied.[*]

Ginga Don was left to retrieve every single ball, a job he carried out with relish. It was an honour to field against the greatest cricketing master in the entire universe.

Her Ladyship led the cheering for what she thought was a wonderful over by her husband. 'It's sheer perfection,' she explained to the wives. 'My husband has just got thirty-six runs, which is the most he can get with his six balls.'

The harem wives applauded. 'You are very lucky to have a husband with six balls,' wife number one said. 'Why you should also want our husband as well is a mystery to us all.'

'But I don't want him anymore,' said Her Ladyship. 'Sir Sidney is the man for me.'

[*]Garfield Sobers was the first batsman to hit six successive sixes off one over in a first-class cricket match, playing for Notts against Glamorgan at Swansea in 1968.

'With six balls,' said number one wife, 'I am not surprised.'

The short-sighted ordnance officer, Second Lieutenant Bendover, set some sort of record of his own by bowling six successive no-balls before he was taken off. He kept running away from the wicket, and bowling the ball towards the boundary. He was finally taken out of the attack when he was no balled for bowling at an ice cream seller in the crowd.

'He's been no-balled,' Her Ladyship explained to the wives.

'Poor man,' said number one wife. 'He is the first eunuch that I have seen playing cricket. No doubt he will now become a guard in our harem.'

The Khasi's XI 175 for no wicket, Ranjitsinhji 150 not out and 24 extras.

At last the ball was tossed to Ginga Don, whose first delivery bowled the Khasi round his legs. Ginga Don threw himself at his feet apologising, but the Khasi felt he had been at the wicket long enough and achieved great things for his team with his one run. Many of his supporters shared his view, and they carried him off shoulder high. There was a delay of ten minutes while umpire Khasiunkh helped in parading him around the ground on his shoulders.

The Khasi's XI 175 for one, Ranjitsinhji 150 not out and 24 extras.

Ginga Don took three more wickets in his sensational first over, including the first hat-trick of the match and without a run being added. The Barmy Army were reawakened, and chanted, 'Ding Dong, Ginga

Don...We're going to Wembley, we shall not be moved.'

Her Ladyship told the wives that Ginga Don had got himself a hat-trick, and could make his balls spin out of the back of his hand.

'That is a trick that the Khasi is always asking me to perform,' said wife number one.

Ginga Don was embarrassed by his success, and hid his face behind his fan. Lieutenant Grimcock shook him by the hand. 'Well done, little Sooty,' he said. 'We might even let you off fanwallahing duties between overs provided you can keep this up.'

'You are a most gracious and kind Lieutenant Grimcock, Sir,' said Ginga Don, and then begged silent forgiveness of his gods because he did not really mean what he said. In truth he thought that the arrogant, supercilious, snobbish Grimcock represented all that was worst about the British and that he should be dropped into a nest of pythons for a long cuddle. But he was far too well-mannered and polite to show such feelings to a man who was a guest in his country.

He salaamed to the Lieutenant, who watched him contemptuously with his hands on his hips. 'What funny people you are,' he said. 'Not at all British. We have got a lot of educating to do in this country before you all know how to behave properly.'

'You are most kind,' said Ginga Don.

The Khasi's XI 175 for four, Ranjitsinhji 150 not out and 24 extras.

The Great Ranjitsinhji knew he needed to get a move on before Ginga Don ran through the rest of the batsmen, and he scored twenty off the next over loosely

145

bowled by Jock McKnacker who putted the ball from his shoulder like he had seen in the Highland Games. Every time his kilt swirled in the following breeze a buzz of excited chatter went round the ground. What, everybody was wondering, did this Scotsman wear under his kilt? They soon found out when, after the Barmy Army had started teasing him with chants of 'Scotland reject' he bent over and invented mooning.

The Great Ranjintsinhji took a mighty swing at the final delivery of McKnacker's over, and the ball flew straight at Captain Ffortescue-Ffortescue and struck him a fearful blow on the head.

Sergeant-Major Thomas came sprinting on with the bucket and sponge, and threw the contents of the bucket, including the remains of a lobster he had been eating, into the Captain's face. He came round and wondered why he had a cracked lobster's claw inside his shirt collar.

'Goodness gracious, what on earth is this lobster doing in my shirt collar?' he asked.

'Why, it's a miracle, Sir' said the Sergeant-Major. 'You're not talking in reverse anymore. It was a cricket ball what did crock you in in the first place, and it is a cricket ball what has cured you.'

That was the good news. The bad news was that the Captain was now completely loopy.

'Help me up, Auntie Matilda,' he said to the Sergeant-Major. 'I've got to do my prep work, and then go with Mummy to pick some flowers.'

The Sergeant-Major helped the Captain back to the pavilion, and Private Tompkins was called out of the

Barmy Army to field in his place.

The Khasi's XI 195 for four, Ranjitsinhji 170 not out and 24 extras.

Ginga Don's deadly spin bowling accounted for another three wickets in his second over, and he had now taken seven wickets for no runs.

The Khasi sent out a message for Ginga Don with his team's ninth batsman. 'The Khasi sends his warmest felicitations,' he said to him quietly in Hindu. 'Provided you take no more wickets, he will pay you one hundred rupees when the game is over and won.'

Ginga Don was most offended. 'But that would not be cricket,' he said. 'Have you not heard of playing up, playing up and playing the game?'

The Khasi's XI 195 for seven, Ranjitsinhji 170 not out and 24 extras. Ginga Don 7-0.

For the first time, there was a hint of desperation in the batting of the Great Ranjitsinhji. He had yet to face a ball from Ginga Don, and he scored another twenty runs off an over of perfectly legitimate underarm deliveries from Scratchwell-Smith. The Khasi's XI needed four more runs to tie and five to win.

'There's a chap bowling his balls under-arm,' Her Ladyship reported to the harem wives, who were not allowed to look because of their purdah.

'My goodness and a night of a thousand stars,' said wife number one. 'That must be awfully painful.'

Umpire Khasiunkh was cursing to himself because he could not get down to Ginga Don's end to call a few no balls, and to curtail his wicket-taking menace. He had his one million rupees bet to worry about. Brother

Belcher felt privileged to see such bowling from Ginga Don and such batting from the Great Ranjitsinhji. 'What great Smellyvision this would make,' he thought.

The Khasi's XI 215 for seven, Ranjitsinhji 190 not out and 24 extras. Ginga Don 7-0.

The bewildering spin of Ginga Don accounted for batsmen nine and ten with the first two balls of his next over, the ninth wicket falling to a comfortable catch to point. While the ball was in the air the batsmen crossed. No run, but the next delivery was to be to the Great Ranjitsinhji, with the last man at the opposite wicket. Still four more runs needed to tie, five to win.

Ginga Don suddenly went numb as he looked down the wicket at his greatest idol. He salaamed to him before running in to bowl, his fingers feeling strangely stiff and his heart beating at three times normal speed. The first loose ball of his spell was immediately punished by the Great Ranjitsinhji, who cut it to the mid-off boundary for four.

The scores were tied.

'Thank you for the honour of striking me to the boundary, oh great and mighty master of cricket,' Ginga Don called down the wicket.

The Great Ranjitsinhji doffed his cap.

Sir Sidney braced himself in the slips. He was sober enough to know that the next ball could decide the fate of his wife and his marriage. The Khasi sat calmly in the pavilion, convinced that the fanwallah was about to sell the match for one hundred rupees. Mudyard Tipling, the world's worst poet, was writing a profound poem about it. Captain Ffortescue-Ffortescue sat alongside Sergeant-Major Thomas wondering why Auntie Matilda had grown a military moustache. Her Ladyship could not understand what was happening. Something about a tie, a last wicket and a crucial ball coming up. All balls were crucial to her mind.

Ginga Don was just about to bowl that crucial ball when there was the sound of the thunder of hooves behind him. He turned to see the unmistakable figure of Bunghit Din galloping across the cricket field on Captain Ffortescue-Ffortescue's white charger. The crowd roared with a mixture of amazement and amusement, thinking it was part of the day's entertainment.

Her Ladyship clapped her hands together. 'Look,' she shouted to the harem wives in excitement, 'they have brought a horse on to play. He's got the biggest balls I've ever seen.'

Forty-seven wives forgot purdah and took a peep.

Sergeant-Major Thomas, sensing danger, stood up. Captain Ffortescue-Ffortescue pointed at the charger speeding right across the cricket pitch. 'Look Auntie Matilda,' he said. 'It's my lovely gee-gee.'

Bunghit Din rode around to the side of the pavilion, and snatched the applauding Lady Ruff-Diamond off her dais and folded her face down across the horse. Then he galloped off in the direction of Fort Phucka.

Her Ladyship was nearly fainting with excitement. What a wonderful game, this cricket.

Mudyard Tipling
A self portrait

A CRICKET QUANDARY

The Battle of the Fort was fought
Without a prisoner being taken,
But Her Ladyship has been caught,
And everybody is now shaken.
The game is standing all square,
One run or a wicket to decide all;
But now she is no longer there,
Should they bowl another ball?

Mudyard Tipling
British India, 1900

150

9

It was agreed with some reluctance to abandon the cricket match as a draw. The Great Ranjitsinhji and Ginga Don shared the man-of-the-match award, a four-foot high elephant fashioned in solid silver. Many considered it much more appealing than the major prize of Her Ladyship. Ginga Don was allowed to touch the award, and the Great Ranjitsinhji took it home. Now, what to do about the main match trophy?

Bunghit Din had ridden off with it, or rather her, like the wind before any of the Khasi's guards could react. Little did they know that they would have faced torture of the most painful kind – a pair of pythons wrapped around the thighs – if they had rescued Her Ladyship. As far as the Khasi was concerned, Bunghit Din should have been given the man-of-the-match award. The *Kalabar Chronicle* captured the drama with a front page banner headline that read: SNATCH OF THE DAY.

Lieutenant Grimcock had assumed command of the 4th Foot and Mouth Regiment because, quite frankly, Captain Ffortescue-Ffortescue was in no fit shape to lead a teddy bear's picnic let alone battle-weary soldiers who were going to need to be motivated into recapturing Fort Phucka.

The Captain was being looked after by the harem wives, and was telling them about a puff-puff train that he had got for Christmas. He cried when the Sergeant-Major left him to shake some life back into the Barmy

Army. 'Auntie Matilda naughty,' he said through sobs. 'Mater and Pater are in the Bahamas and now she has left me.' Number one wife cuddled him, and Auntie Matilda was quickly forgotten.

No sense whatsoever could be got out of the Governor. He thought that the galloping white charger was an addition to the pink elephants that he had been seeing lately, and he was now deep into a gin-generated sleep in the pavilion dressing-room.

It was a wonder he had not been awakened by the roars of the Sergeant-Major. 'Right, boyhos,' he yelled at the sullen Barmy Army. 'Get fell in. We is going to march back to Fort Phucka and recapture it from the revolting Burpas.'

'Permission to speak, Sir,' said Private Arden, raising a hand.

'What is it boyho?' said the Sergeant-Major, peering at Arden with his most threatening stare. 'This is no time for any of your bloody stupid questions.'

'I was just wondering,' said Arden, 'if it's all right for Private McKnacker and me, like, to be marching in our cricket whites.'

'Well as your battle dress is back in the Fort,' said the Sergeant-Major, 'it will have to be all right, won't it? Don't think you're going to get out of this battle just because you're dressed like a couple of pansies in that ridiculous cricket ge...'

The words died in the Sergeant-Major's throat as Lieutenant Grimcock marched purposefully to the front of the parade dressed in pristine cricketing whites, and with a silk, striped cravat around his neck. He was

152

carrying his cricket bat as he would a rifle.

Sergeant-Major Thomas was just a little concerned about the way the Lieutenant was rapidly blinking every two minutes or so. It was the classic shell-shock symptoms that he had often seen soldiers suffering after battle, and he had noticed it had started when the Great Ranjitsinhji had hit him for five successive boundaries off his one and only over.

'I'll address the men, Sergeant-Major,' he said, 'if you would bring them to order.'

For Lieutenant Montague Grimcock this was a dream come true. He had always wanted to command a regiment since, as a schoolboy at Eton, reading of the exploits of Wellington at Waterloo. All right, so the 4th Foot and Mouth paraded before him now – some in kilts, others in cricketing whites, O'Shaughnessy in baseball uniform and the Sergeant-Major in his rugby shirt and shorts – did not exactly look the sort of crack outfit that the Duke of Wellington was able to call on, but he was ready to demand that they do their best for Queen and country. Wars, so it was said, were won on the playing fields of Eton. Grimcock was ready to play up, play up and play the game, and to give the Burpas a jolly good thrashing. If only he could control this bloody blinking that made him feel as if he was continually looking at the world through Venetian blinds.

'Parade, 'shun!' roared the Sergeant-Major. 'And put down them bloody beer crates.'

The Barmy Army pulled itself to the best attention they could manage in the circumstances. They had been supping beer all day long in boiling heat, and the thought of a ten-mile march back to the Fort and then a battle to recapture it was not exactly filling them with enthusiasm.

Grimcock decided to appeal to their *esprit de corps*. 'I am only a recent recruit to this regiment,' he said, 'but I am already aware of the great camaraderie and regimental pride that exists. As Wellington said on the eve of battle at Waterloo, "Now is the time for all good men to come to the aid of the party, and kick Froggie arse".'

Sergeant-Major Thomas was a keen student of military history and could not recall that exact quote, but he was prepared to accept that his superior officer knew what he was talking about.

'We have a two-fold task ahead of us,' said Grimcock. 'First we must recapture Fort Phucka from the revolting Burpas, and then we will make every effort to find Her Ladyship. What has happened here today is enough to make the blood of every true Brit boil.'

Ginga Don, fanning him for all he was worth, nodded his head vigorously.

'To be robbed of victory by a bowler who cheated by tampering with the ball is just not on,' said Grimcock, seething with anger. 'Then, to cap it all, some blighter comes and kidnaps the Governor's wife. Well now they've got our dander up, and they're jolly well going to pay for it.'

'Year, year,' said the Sergeant-Major.

Grimcock smartly presented arms with his cricket bat. 'Over to you, Sergeant-Major,' he said. 'We must quick march on the Fort. I want us to hit them at sundown before that bounder Napoleon has had time to have his brandy.'

Sergeant-Major Thomas pretended he had not heard that last sentence. 'Right, boyhos,' he roared, 'by the left, quick march.'

The Barmy Army, led by the two pipers flanking the Lieutenant and the Sergeant-Major, marched away from the ground with the exception of one soldier. Short-sighted ordnance officer Bendover had marched off in the wrong direction, and Ginga Don was sent to show him the way.

Mudyard Tipling went along to write about it, and Brother Belcher to pray. 'One day,' he prophesied, looking at his palms, 'soldiers will not have to march into battle but will be transported by huge gun-carrying vehicles called wanks, and news of the battles will be relayed back to HQ by facts machines.'

'What do your palms tell you about my future poems?' asked Tipling, as they prepared to tag along with the Barmy Army.

'It says very clearly,' said Brother Belcher, looking closely at his palms, 'that they will continue to be utter crap.'

Tipling did not speak another word to him on the road to Kalabar.

As the Barmy Army marched away, the Governor was still sound asleep in the dressing-room, oblivious to what was going on. Captain Ffortescue-Ffortescue was teaching the harem wives 'Baa Baa Black Sheep', and the Khasi was celebrating the kidnapping of Her Ladyship by insisting that they go ahead with the

155

fireworks display that had originally been meant only to mark a victory by his team.

This, thought the Khasi, is a victory of sorts. He would remember to send Bunghit Din a herd of goats as a thank you gesture if the revolting Burpas leader survived this night.

Bunghit Din had arrived back at the Fort with his prize. He just avoided a rupture as he lifted Her Ladyship down off the horse, and then dismounted and walked around her like an art critic inspecting a sculpture.

'Am I in or out?' she asked, giggling. 'My you are a big boy for your mummy, aren't you?'

'And you're a bit of all right, too,' said Bunghit Din, who now realised why she was the trophy for the winner of the cricket match. He liked his women with a bit of flesh on them, and this one had lots and lots of it.

'Come, oh wonderful jewel of the west,' he said. 'We have some curried lamb left over. Please let me prepare you a great feast before I decide just what we should do with you.'

Her Ladyship was very puzzled and also a little excited. 'Do with me?' she said. 'I say, am I going to get an innings, and will you show me your famous swingers?'

Bunghit Din shook his head in amazement. The forwardness of these western women made his turban throb and stand on end, which was a euphemism only a Burpa would understand.

She still thought it was all part and parcel of the cricket match, and was pleasantly surprised at the

156

complexities of a game that she had always looked on as about as exciting as watching grass grow. She did not realise that the game extended off the pitch to take in horse riding.

The ride on the white charger had been the sort of thing erotic dreams are made of. She had leant back on the strong, silent horseman and enjoyed the rhythm of the ride with him as she hung on to his powerful thighs. Who wanted the sullen Khasi or the sozzled Sir Sidney when she could fold herself into the muscular arms of a big hunk like this?

Bunghit Din had been furious on his return to find that he had lost another three hundred tribesmen. They had been the change of guard, and had been shot by the old guard when reporting for duty. 'It was,' explained a five-star general, 'one of those unfortunate accidents. Perhaps, in hindsight, it had been unwise to use the password "shoot".'

But with five hundred good fighting men left, and Her Ladyship as a most valuable and sought-after hostage Bunghit Din was very confident that they could hold the Fort against an attack that he expected at the first light of day.

He told the remains of his troops, 'Prepare for the father of all battles.'

'Pardon me, great and all-knowing leader,' said one of his generals, 'but do you not mean the "mother" of all battles?'

'I am not prepared to waste time arguing the parentage,' he said. 'I have far more important things to do before battle commences.'

157

Bunghit Din looked at Her Ladyship swathed in her see-through veils and he felt his turban rising.

To keep their spirits up as they marched, Queen Victoria's Barmy Army sang parodies of songs that were waiting to be composed. 'I Left My Fart in San Francisco' was a favourite, as was 'Pissed Again, As We Were Last Summer'. Ginga Don marched at the front for a spell, while they all sang 'My Old Man Said Follow the Fan', and then he himself performed on the current number one in the Indian charts, 'The Sari With the Fringe on Top'. Jock McKnacker, accompanied by the bagpipes, gave an enthusiastic and moving rendition of 'When I've had a couple of drinks on a Saturday, India belongs to me'.

Sergeant-Major Thomas, of course, lent his booming Welsh bass voice to each song, and won applause for his solo performance of 'Bread of Devon, knead me 'til I want no more'. Sean O'Shaughnessy sang the beautiful ballad dedicated to Irish plumbers, 'Oh Danny Boy, the pipes the pipes are overflowing'. The only time there was any dissent was when Brother Belcher tried to sing, 'Onward Muslim Soldiers'. Mudyard Tipling pitched in with 'On the Road to Kalabar', which was based on Kipling's Road to Mandalay, and Scratchwell-Smith sang a song that he had learned at his Russian grandmother's knee, 'Wrap Up Your Roubles in Your Old Kitbag and Smile, Smile, Smile.'

Lieutenant Grimcock was quite stuffy at first, but then after a little elbow-nudging encouragement from the Sergeant-Major joined in and sang 'The Eton

Boating Song', which did not go down too well with the ranks. He began to wonder if it was not perhaps all getting a little bit out of hand as the Barmy Army started to conga down the road to Kalabar.

Spirits were high when the Fort came into view, and so as not to alert the Burpas the Lieutenant requested that they sing pianissimo. It was Private Arden who said, 'You hum it, and we'll sing along.' They settled for a quiet version of the naval song 'I Was Born Under a Wandering Tar', with the Sergeant-Major's bass voice ideal for the lead, and Ginga Don providing a very decent descant.

The worried lookout on duty at Fort Phucka reported urgently to Bunghit Din. 'Sir, there are strange noises reaching my ears,' he said.

'Yes,' said Bunghit Din. 'They are all around the Fort. A touch too much curry in the lamb stew I fancy.'

He then returned his attentions to the desirous Ladyship. She was lying back on a pallet made of old orange boxes, with her eyes peeping romantically out above her yashmak and her fleshy thighs showing teasingly beneath her seven veils. The spartan barracks room was not quite as comfortable and as richly furnished as the harem, but Her Ladyship considered that it had a certain sexual ambience that was lacking at the pristine palace. She felt it was best summed up as raw and randy.

'Your eyes, your Ladyship,' said Bunghit Din, 'are like the stars of the heavens, and your hair is as the silken strands of a goddess. Your ears feel like the pearls of paradise, and your neck is that of the most elegant of wondrous flamingos.'

She let her yashmak fall. Bunghit Din took one look at what he had heard Englishmen describe as 'the boat race' and pulled the yashmak back into place. 'Oh well,' he thought silently to himself, 'she can't have everything.'

'What happens next?' asked her Ladyship, wondering whether he was going to bring his new balls out. 'Will you be batting or bowling?'

Bunghit Din, perhaps not surprisingly, looked puzzled.

'In or out?' she said.

'Both, eventually,' said Bunghit Din, 'but I think a little more foreplay is called for first of all.'

'Four or six,' said Her Ladyship. 'I'm game, if you are.'

Bunghit Din was confused by this western talk. He had heard of a sixty-nine but never a four and six.

'When this bloody war is over...' he said.

'Oh, it's just a game,' she said, 'although the master playwright George Bernard Shaw will one day say that sport between nations is just a substitute for war.'

'...I will build you your very own Taj Mahal, with a silver-encrusted roof, gold-tiled flooring and diamond-studded walls.'

'Can I also have a lean-to?' she said. 'I always like a bit on the side.'

'But, of course,' said Bunghit Din. 'There will be nothing I will not do for my precious, precocious princess.'

'Just a Lady, I'm afraid,' said Her Ladyship, blushing

160

beneath her yashmak while down below her veils her thighs were yearning.

'But when this bloody war is over...'

'Game,' corrected her Ladyship, putting two fingers gently to his lips. He kissed them, trying not to notice the strong lamb curry flavour. He was fuming when they had to eat without cutlery because of the earlier carnage in the dining hall.

'When it's over,' he continued, 'I will make you my princess. I will worship you hand and foot, and will kiss every inch of you all the way from the tops of your fingers to the tips of your toes.'

'Be careful when you're kissing my toes,' said Her Ladyship.

'How do you mean?' said Bunghit Din.

'Well make sure there are none of those new-style photographers around,' she said. 'Brother Belcher saw a princess getting a toe job in his tea leaves the other day, and he said it nearly brings the Queen down. Poor old Victoria, God bless her.'

'Tell me, my wonderful jewel of the west,' said Bhungit Dun, 'what is the one thing you would like me to do for you that would make you the happiest person in the entire universe?'

Her Ladyship refrained from stating the obvious because she was sure she was going to get that anyway, judging by the way his scabbard was rising.

'Let me think,' she said. 'I have always dreamed of having a wine lake of my very own.'

'Count that as done,' he said. 'In the grounds of our private palace you will have a lake of wine. No, not just

161

one but three. One of red, one of white and one of pink champagne.'

'I don't like to pry,' lied Her Ladyship, 'but you must be awfully rich to afford all these things. There must be a lot of money in revolting.'

'I am not yet rich rich,' he admitted, 'but between you, me and this bedpost I soon will be.'

'What, when this bloody game is over?' she said.

The Burpas leader looked around to make sure nobody was eavesdropping. The three hundred tribesmen in the barracks were obviously fast asleep because their chorus of snoring was enough to wake the dead.

'I will share a secret with you, my flower of the heavens,' he whispered.

Her Ladyship dipped her head forward to try to hear above the snores, and butted him on the nose.

'I'm sorry, tweetiepie,' she said.

'Do not worry about it,' said Bunghit Din, staunching the stream of blood trickling down his nose with the cuff of his sleeve. 'That is like the kiss of thunder. It makes me really excited.'

'Ye, gods,' thought Her Ladyship. 'He must really like it rough.'

'What's the great secret?' she said aloud.

He bent close and whispered into her ear. 'I know where the Khasi's treasure is hidden,' he said, 'and before the night is through I shall have it away.'

'I hope,' said Her Ladyship, 'that you mean *we* will have it away.'

Bunghit Din kissed her on the forehead, licking where some of the lamb stew had got entwined in her silk headdress. 'Of course, my golden love dove,' he said. 'We will have it away together.'

Her Ladyship removed one of her veils and mopped her perspiring brow. Just six more veils to go, and she was not going to need to dance to strip them off. This new tall, dark and gruesome man in her life could take care of that with one snatch of his sausage-fingered hands. She could not wait to say the magic words, 'Bung it in, Bunghit Din.'

Meanwhile, back at the cricket ground, Sir Sidney was just coming out of his deep sleep. He had a hangover that could be measured in fathoms, and his throat felt as tight and dry as, to quote a common cliché of the time, Elizabeth the First's pussy (apparently a mean cat that never needed a drink).

'Where the hell has everybody gone?' he asked the groundsman, Ali Grassmowa, who was waiting to lock up the dressing-room.

'They've gone to their graveyards, every one,' he replied, shaking his head sadly. 'When will they ever learn? When will they ever learn?'

'What are you chuntering on about, man?' said Sir Sidney, talking above the hammering in his head. 'What happened in the cricket match? Who won?'

'It was a most honourable tie,' said Ali. 'The Great Ranjitsinhji gloriously made all the running, and the fantastical fanwallah Ginga Don bowled his balls most beautifully. Never have such wonderul things been seen on a cricket field.'

'So what's happened to the prize?'

'It was shared, sahib Sir,' said Ali, 'between the Great Ranjitsinhji and Ginga Don.'

Sir Sidney coughed and spluttered, and he suddenly felt as if the entire Barmy Army was marching through his aching head. 'They're sharing my wife?' he said despairingly.

'Goodness gracious, no,' said Ali. 'You must mean the match prize.'

'Of course I bloody do, you great silly groundwallah you.'

'That's most kind of you, sahib Sir, to call me a great groundwallah,' said Ali, bowing his turbaned head. 'I do my best, but it is not easy when the rain it does not come too often. I would have preferred today to have had just a little more moisture in the pitch. But then, perhaps it would not have suited the batting of the Great Ranjitsinhji or the bowling of Ginga Don quite so much, sahib Sir.'

'What the bloody hell has happened to my wife?' Sir Sidney managed to roar through a gradually loosening throat.

'Ah, she has gone off with the horseman,' said Ali.

'The horseman?' said Sir Sidney, conjuring in his mind an image of a beast that was half man, half horse (which was not too far removed from an identikit of Bunghit Din).

'Yes,' explained Ali. 'It was a wonderful climax to a wonderful game. He came on his splendid white charger and swept Her Ladyship off her feet. I just wish he had not made so many hoof marks on my pitch. It is going to be a devil of a job to remove them, even with the big roller that is pulled by our strongest elephant. This will mean the pitch becoming lower and flatter and so taking even more spin.'

It was Sir Sidney's mind that was in a spin. He had vague recollections of seeing a white horse galloping across the cricket field, but thought it was part of the gin-induced demons who had been haunting him ever since Lady Ruff-Diamond had left him to join the cunning Khasi.

'Where have Captain Ffortescue-Ffortescue and the Foot and Mouth Regiment gone?' he asked.

'Ah, good old Queen Victoria's, God bless Her, Barmy Army have gone to recapture Fort Phucka,' Ali said, 'and the Captain has gone to the harem.'

'We'll soon see about that,' said Sir Sidney. 'If he thinks he can enjoy himself in a bloody harem while his men are going into battle he has another think coming.'

There was no transport around, and so Ali Grassmowa gave the Governor a lift to the nearby palace in his wheelbarrow.

Guards stopped him charging straight into the harem where the Khasi's wives were being serenaded by Captain Ffortescue-Ffortescue to a medley of nursery rhymes.

The Khasi was told about the Governor's appearance at the gateway to the harem, forbidden territory to all but the castrated guards and specially invited guests who needed to be personally vetted, and sometimes neutered, by the Khasi.

He was not quite so antagonistic towards the Governor now that he was rid of his dreadful wife, but he had a new nuisance on his hands in the shape of the potty Captain Ffortescue-Ffortescue. His wives had adopted him like a small child, and while his influence was not as vindictive as Her Ladyship's there was certainly only so much he could take of 'Baa Baa Black Sheep', 'Jack and Jill' and 'The Queen of Hearts' who apparently baked some bloody tarts.

'Ah, Sir Sidney,' he said, bowing in greeting, and then using a phrase he had picked up at Oxford, 'what can I do you for?'

'Well for a start,' said an irate Sir Sidney, 'you can tell me where my wife is, and for another you can let me inside these gates so that I can tell that no-good Captain Ffortescue-Ffortescue that he should get back to his duty to Queen and country this instant.'

'Regarding question number one,' said the Khasi, 'I wish I could help you, but I have not seen hide or hair of your good lady wife since she was kidnapped by the revolting Burpa leader Bunghit Din.'

'But what would he want with my wife?' asked Sir Sidney.

'One of such rare beauty brings out the demon in men,' he replied.

'You should know,' said Sir Sidney. 'You couldn't keep your bloody bejewelled mitts off her.'

'A thousand thousand pardons for the vexation that I have caused you, oh noble Governor of Her Majesty Queen Victoria's province of Kalabar,' he said, salaaming as he made his abject apology. 'I can only assure you from my deepest bottom that the magnetic attraction I had for your wife was not a deliberate

166

impulse over which I had control. However, I was prepared to do all in my power to return her to you virtually unsullied, but I have to tell you in all humility that it was she who insisted that our relationship continue.'

'All right, get up off your knees and leave my feet alone,' said an embarrassed Sir Sidney, who hated to see grown men grovel. 'Now let me in to see the Captain.'

'I will do that, gracious Governor,' the Khasi said, 'but I must forewarn your mightiness that he is not quite the same Captain that so bravely led his regiment into the siege at Mafeking.'

'What d'you mean?' said Sir Sidney. 'You haven't had him eunuched, have you?'

'No, nothing that drastic,' he said, 'although he did volunteer for the treatment. It is not his balls that have been castrated as much as his brains.'

He ushered Sir Sidney into the harem where the Governor used to clandestinely spend many titillating hours before the spoilsport Khasi tightened up on his security. As he followed the Khasi in he could hardly believe his ears. The Captain was saying aloud in a little-boy voice, 'Twinkle, twinkle little star... how I wonder what you are...'

'Captain Ffortescue-Ffortescue,' he shouted, making the wives jump and cover their ears.

The Captain looked at the Governor with contempt. 'Go away, you naughty man,' he said. 'You have frightened the baby-sitters. You will be in trouble with Mater and Pater when they return from the South of

France. And Auntie Matilda will be furious, and will send you to bed without supper.'

Sir Sidney was astonished on two counts; one, that he could understand what the Captain was saying, and two, that he appeared to have reverted to his childhood.

'What about your duty to Queen and country?' he said, already resigned to the fact that he was wasting his time talking to the little boy lost in front of him.

'The Queen of Hearts, she baked some tarts...'

'All on a summer's day,' chorused the wives.

'He has been like this since that unfortunate incident when the cricket ball hit him on his head,' said the Khasi. 'I am afraid I must ask you to take him with you before he further corrupts my wives with his evil thoughts.'

'Evil?' said Sir Sidney. 'What d'you mean, evil? Sounds to me as if everything he is spouting is as innocent as springtime.'

'Oh no, Sir Sidney, on the contrary,' said the Khasi. 'Just an hour ago he was trying to coax my number one wife to put her pussy in the well, and he asked number two wife to come blow his horn. This is a child monster, and I want him out of my harem. Now!'

He clapped his hands, and two armed-to-the-teeth guards appeared as if out of trap doors either side of the Captain. They roughly pulled him away from the wives, and handed him over to the Khasi, who quite frankly would have been happy never to clap eyes on him again, although he would liked to have heard the whole of 'Jack and Jill' to see if there was a happy ending.

The wives wept as if losing a child of their own as Sir Sidney and the crying Captain were shown the way out.

168

Two camels had been saddled, and the Khasi pointed the way to Fort Phucka. 'Just keep following the road to Kalabar,' he said. 'You should arrive there within the hour.'

The guards helped the Governor and the Captain mount the camels, and then whipped their behinds to send them galloping on their way. What the Governor could not understand was why they did not whip the camels.

'Am I going to ride this cockhorse all the way to Banbury Cross?' the Captain called across to the Governor in his little boy voice. The Governor ignored him because he had all his concentration on holding on for dear life to the camel's neck as they bounced along a rutted path that passed for a road.

Behind them, the Khasi ordered the start of the fireworks display. He now had two things to celebrate: the kidnapping of Her Ladyship and the departure of the loony Captain. It was quite appropriate that he should return to lead the Barmy Army.

The first rocket soared into the night sky and came back down to ground, still flaming, right in front of the Captain's camel, who reared with fright and threw Ffortescue-Ffortescue backwards to the rutted path. He landed on his head.

Sir Sidney dismounted with great difficulty, and raced over to where the Captain lay in a heap. He slowly opened his eyes as the Governor bent over him. 'What the hucking fell was that?' he said. 'I thought I'd chad my hips then.'

Sir Sidney found himself hugging the Captain. 'You're back to abnormal,' he said. 'Good old Captain

169

Ffortescue-Ffortescue.'

'Get off, you lilly sump,' said the Captain, pushing the Governor away. 'This is not time for saft dentiment. We must Fort the free and find your Shadylip.'

They remounted the camels and galloped off towards Fort Phucka.

The final battle of Fort Phucka was all over by the time the Governor and the Captain arrived. It went down in the annals of warfare as one of the strangest battles ever fought. Relatively speaking, it was not a mother and a father of a battle; more little brother. The soldiers of the 4th Foot and Mouth Regiment did not fire a single bullet.

With a self-destruct skill unique to them, the Burpas managed to polish themselves off within the confines of the Fort walls. They had started firing the moment one of the Khasi's three-stage rockets had lit up the night sky above the Fort, but they forgot the fairly basic fact that they should have fired at targets on the *other* side of the wall.

Many of them had come running from their beds, rifles in hand, only to be shot down by their fellow tribesmen, who had been taught to recognise them by the names on their shirts. The fact that they did not have their shirts on after being startled out of their sleep meant there was no way of identifying them. It was during this battle that the popular saying was first launched, 'Keep your shirt on!'

The Foot and Mouth marksmen lay with their Enfield rifles pointed at the Fort ready to open fire, but they did not catch a glimpse of the enemy let alone see the whites of their eyes. Lieutenant Grimcock, swishing his cricket bat around like a sword, was convinced it was some kind of a trap. He tried to think what his idol, the Iron Duke, would have done in similar circumstances, and first of all he changed his boots and put on wellingtons.

He found Privates Arden and McKnacker digging themselves in, and joined them in their trench. 'I don't like this, men,' he said.

'Well it's not the Savoy,' said Arden, 'but it's the best we can do in the circumstances.'

'No,' snapped the Lieutenant, his blink now going so rapidly that he felt as if he were watching one of those magic lantern shows that had become all the rage on the County house circuit back home. 'What I mean is I don't like the fact that we can hear but cannot see the enemy.'

'Well it suits me fine,' said Arden, crouching lower in the trench 'the only thing I'm concerned about is that they don't see me.'

'But why on earth would they be shooting *inside* the Fort when we are out here?' said the Lieutenant, more to himself than to these two cretins who were obviously interested only in survival. He was quite prepared to go right up to the Fort wall to see what was going on, but he knew he could not count on their support.

'Och, it's obvious what's going on,' said Jock McKnacker, as he casually cleaned trench dirt out of his nails with the point of his dirk.

'What's obvious?' chorused the Lieutenant and Private Arden.

171

'They're banging away in there,' said McKnacker, 'knowing that eventually some daft Lieutenant will go right up tae the Fort wall to see what's going on, and then they'll blow his heed off.'

The Lieutenant pretended that he did not hear him, and started trying to think of an alternative plan. They lay listening to the gun fire and above it all they thought they could hear a wailing, moaning sound like a cow in labour. In actual fact, it was Her Ladyship's battle cry as she at last got Bunghit Din to lower his pantaloons.

By the time Bunghit Din had pulled himself away from the passionate clutches of Her Ladyship the damage had been done. There was only one Burpa warrior left when he came running into the Fort square, and this sole survivor had his head split open by a devastating hook shot from Lieutenant Grimcock, who led his Barmy Army in through the virtually unguarded gates waving his cricket bat and shouting: 'Not tonight, Napoleon!'

Bunghit Din quickly summed up the situation, and decided he should scarper pretty damn quick. He raced back to where Her Ladyship was reclining on the orange box pallet, wondering if the earth had moved for her or whether she had been hearing rifle shots. The Burpas leader grabbed her roughly by the arm and yanked her to her feet. 'Ah, the rough stuff,' she thought. 'I guessed he would get round to it.'

'Come,' he said. 'You're my insurance. We're going to get the treasure and then I shall decide what to do with you.'

He put her over his shoulder (a feat that in itself

172

deserved a medal), grabbed his rifle and a shovel and raced through the secret passages to where he had tethered the white charger in case of an emergency getaway such as this. He had known all about the secret ins and outs of Fort Phucka since it was first designed by a Burpa architect, who tragically tripped up and fell on his ceremonial sword at the opening ceremony.

Lieutenant Grimcock, Captain Ffortescue-Ffortescue and Sir Sidney came dashing into the barracks room just after Bunghit Din had made his escape with his prize. Her Ladyship was ecstatic. Will this game of cricket never end?

'The camned dad has rone a dunner,' said the Captain, who, much to Grimcock's undisguised disappointment, had resumed command. 'And the Sirty dwine has taken Her Shadylip with him.'

Sir Sidney wondered if perhaps he might have preferred the nursery rhymes.

A body count showed that four hundred Burpa warriors had died during the Battle of Fort Phucka. This surprised the Lieutenant, because intelligence reports suggested that there were five hundred tribesmen left to defend the Fort.

An inch-by-inch search of the Fort solved the mystery. The remaining hundred Burpa tribesmen were found alive and unwell slumped on toilet seats.

They had been the only victims of the Great Curry Powder Plot.

Mudyard Tipling
A self portrait

TAKEN FOR A RIDE

Her Ladyship thinks it is all part of the match
When she is taken off in search of treasure.
She does not realise that there is a catch
And that for her there will be no pleasure.
The revolting Burpa leader is an evil man,
Who is not just taking her along for the ride.
He sees her as part of his escape plan,
While she sees him as her bit on the side.

Mudyard Tipling
British India, 1900

174

10

GOONDHI was sitting cross-legged trying to meditate, but the noise of the Khasi's exploding fireworks combined with the sound of rifle fire from the direction of Fort Phucka made deep contemplation extremely difficult. He got up from his cushion and poured himself another glass of his own urine, which he drank daily because he believed it purified his system and his soul. It made him self sufficient and very regular. Goondhi called it 'having a quick one'.

He had no idea that the Great Curry Powder Plot was doomed to failure because of a chapter of accidents and a disastrous communications hang-up. All his thoughts were centred on how to run India once the British had packed up and gone home to where they belonged.

The first thing he and his committee of wise men would introduce was compulsory meditation. 'We will become the thinking man's country,' he said. Second on the agenda was an end to the unjust Raj system. There would be no more Khasis living off the fat of the land while about them millions of people starved. The days of one man having five hundred servants were numbered. It would be a fairer society, with people judged for what they were as human beings not by caste and religion.

High on the agenda would be the removal of all Queen Victoria's portraits. Millions of Indians had been brainwashed into hanging them in their homes. Now Goondhi planned a great 'Burn the Queen' festival, and he would modestly ask if they would hang his portrait on their walls in her place. He had always secretly wanted to be well hung.

His thoughts of a perfect India were interrupted by a rapping at the door, and Mudyard Tipling came in posing as the man from the *Times*, Mortimer Hacker. He had been sent to interview Goondhi to see if he knew anything about the whereabouts of the kidnapped Lady Ruff-Diamond. It was an assignment that Mudyard, remembering his experiences with Goondhi's animal and reptile relatives, did not relish, but no less a person than the Governor of Kalabar had insisted that the tracking down of Bunghit Din and Her Ladyship should be given top priority.

'Ah, my friend from the *Times*,' said Goondhi, bowing low in greeting. 'Please come in and make yourself at home. I'm afraid you find me on my own. Father is away organising a snake-charming protest meeting.'

That was the good news. Now the bad news.

'My Uncle Akbar will be coming here shortly,' he said. 'I always share my late-night supper with him, a dry biscuit.'

He indicated the flask of urine. 'Can I interest you in a drink – just a quick one, so to speak?'

Mudyard was feeling parched and nothing would go down better than a nice glass of refreshing orange. 'Yes, please,' he said. 'That looks like fresh orange. Just what I could do with.'

'I would say that it is more lemon mixed with a little cocoa that I had last night,' Goondhi said, as he poured

Mudyard a glass. 'I generate it myself.'

He took the drink and sank it with one tilt of his head. He looked at the empty glass and smacked his lips. 'That's better,' he said. 'Just what the doctor ordered. You must give me the recipe before I go. It's nice and tangy, just how I like it.'

Goondhi was back in his cross-legged position on his cushion. 'Now then, my friend, exactly what is it that is so urgent that it has brought you out here at this time of the night?' he asked.

'I'm looking for Lady Ruff-Diamond,' said Mudyard, getting straight to the point because he wanted to escape before his old enemy Akbar appeared.

'I understand that all red-blooded men around here are doing the same thing,' said Goondhi, who had heard all sorts of startling tales about Her Ladyship's dalliances. 'But why would the *Times* be interested in her. Surely they would not buy her story for salacious serialisation?'

'No, it is a news story that I am working on,' said Mudyard. 'She has been kidnapped by Bunghit Din, the leader of the revolting Burpas, and I am making inquires for my newspaper.'

'Bunghit Din, that horrible snake in the grass,' said Goondhi, showing unusual vehemence. 'Do you know I once saw his father win a wrestling match by turning his opponent's testicles into a bow tie knotted around the neck. There is a cruel streak running through that family, and I would be very anxious about Her Ladyship's fate.'

He offered Mudyard a refill of his glass, which he

accepted gratefully.

'So you have no idea where Bunghit Din might be hiding?' he asked.

'Goodness gracious, I would have no idea,' said Goondhi. 'I would run a million miles if I saw him coming anywhere near me. He is a terrible, terrible man. Tell me, what was all that shooting at the Fort earlier this evening?'

'That was the 4th Foot and Mouth Regiment recapturing the Fort from the Burpas,' said Mudyard. 'I have written a poem about it that I would like to read to you...'

Goondhi was saved by the sound of paws scratching at the front door.

'Ah,' he said, 'that will be Uncle Akbar. He will be delighted to see you.'

Mudyard quickly drained his glass and stood up. 'I'm terribly sorry but I must be on my way,' he said. 'I would greatly appreciate it if you could let me know if you see or hear of the whereabouts of Bunghit Din and Her Ladyship.'

He turned at the door. 'By the way, Mr Goondhi,' he said, 'that lemonade has such a unique taste that I recommend that you bottle it. If you are interested, I could set up a franchise business for you. There would, I feel sure, be a great demand for it right around the world.'

Goondhi laughed like a drain. 'I think you English would say that I do not have the bottle for it.' he said. 'I only produce in the wee small hours of the morning.'

'What is the main ingredient?' asked Mudyard,

secretly planning to steal the recipe.

'Piddle, of course,' said Goondhi.

'Piddle?' said Mudyard. 'I don't think I've heard of piddleade.'

'Not piddleade,' said Goondhi. 'Just piddle.'

It had still not registered with Mudyard just what he had been drinking.

'How do you manufacture it?' he asked.

'I just stand in front of the chamber pot and urinate, of course,' said Goondhi, opening the door to let Akbar in and Mudyard out.

As he walked out to the waiting tongawallah with Akbar hanging to his right ankle, Mudyard felt very pissed off.

Bunghit Din arrived back at the cricket ground in the middle of the night. He had hidden out of sight for two hours a mile from Fort Phucka while search parties looked in vain for him and his illustrious hostage. He had Her Ladyship folded over in front of him on the horse, a gag around her mouth to stop her alerting anybody. She also had her ankles and wrists roped together.

Lady Ruff-Diamond had heard somebody say that the cricket match was a tie, and obviously this was part of the tying up process. She had never been so aroused, although she did wish Bunghit Din would show just a little tenderness. He had been throwing her around like a sack of potatoes, and now she was trussed up like a turkey ready for roasting. Or, as she more optimistically thought of it, a jolly good rogering.

Bunghit Din galloped across the deserted cricket field from where he had snatched her nearly ten hours earlier. The leader of the vanishing Burpas knew that this would be the last place that they would think of looking for him. Years of living in darkened caves along the Khyber Pass had given him almost cat-like sight at night, and even though it was pitch black he managed to find his way to the middle of the cricket field where the stumps were still standing at each end of the twenty-two yard long pitch. He lifted Her Ladyship off the horse and lay her down beside the pitch. Her breath was so hot that she was misting up her veils as she watched him return to the horse and remove the shovel that had been tied to the saddle bags. So this was where the cricket match would end, she thought, back at the pitch where it had started. But why the shovel? She wanted him to dig in to her, so to speak, but this was ridiculous.

Bunghit Din walked to the stumps at the far end of the pitch, kicked the shovel into the ground and started digging for all he was worth. His father had told him that the Khasi had buried his treasure beneath the cricket pitch, and now he had come to plunder it.

Her Ladyship watched him digging away, and thought how silly it was that he should be using all that energy when it could have been far more enjoyably used on her. If something did not happen pretty soon in the humping and grunting stakes, she would begin to lose her new-found passion for the game of cricket.

An hour had been wasted by the Foot and Mouth search teams because the ordance officer, the short-sighted Bendover, had given them maps of the Peak District and they had spent precious time bumping into each other in the Khyber Pass while trying to find Kinder Scout and Lake Coniston. Captain Ffortescue-Ffortescue then took personal charge of the hunt, and addressed the full regiment on the parade ground in what he considered his best Churchillian tones (Lord Randolph Churchill, of course): 'I know wery vell that you have all had a diring tay, what with the chrama and dallenge of the micket cratch and then the Fattle of Bucka Fort in which you scored a vagnificent mictory under the temporary but lirring steadership of Lieutenant Cockgrim. But now I am asking you to becharge your ratteries and to redouble your efforts to drack town Dunghit Bin and Her Shiplady. We know they must be within a men tile fadius of the rort, because that old chite wharger of mine can not mavel trore than men tiles without collapsing, particularly when you consider that he is having to forry the carmidable bigure of the Furpas leader and the equally sizeable, if I say may so, Lady Duff-Riamond. The Mergeant-Sajor will organise you into pearch sarties of a mozen den each. You will all be accompanied by borchtearer wallahs who know the tocal lerrain, and I want you to leave no tone unsurned, no crook or nanny unsearched and no hole unplumbed. We owe it to Her Shiplady to find her and bring her hack bome to her hoting dusband. Go to it my wrave barriors. I wish you all the lest of buck. Huppy hanting.'

Never before had one parade ground seen so many gaping mouths. 'What bleeding language was that?'

Private Arden said out of the side of his mouth to Private McKnacker.

'I think that cricket ball must have hit him a few inches below the belt,' said McKnacker. 'He's talking a load of balls.'

Sergeant-Major Thomas decided a quick summary was necessary. 'Right, boyhos,' he roared. 'You've had your horders from the Captain, and I will just rehiterate that yous are to form patrols of a dozen men each and follow your torchbearer wallahs. Search every nook and cranny within a ten-mile radius. We must find Her Ladyship before that revolting Burpa does something very nasty to her.'

The men were fired up at the thought of an Englishwoman, the Governor's wife no less, being at the mercy of a mad dog like Bunghit Din, and they started out on their searches with gusto. But only one of the people on the parade ground guessed exactly where to go to find the Burpa leader.

Bunghit Din was hidden out of sight of Her trussed-up Ladyship. He was up to his turban down the third hole that he had dug in the cricket pitch. The prospect of finding the treasure had given him the strength of six men and great mounds of earth were building up either side of the pitch as he carried out his excavations. Her Ladyship wondered if this was where the saying had come from, 'Did the earth move for you?'

So far Bunghit Din had found nothing apart from a lot of soil and the remains of a body. On closer inspection he found that it was Ali Grassmowa One, the father of the current groundsman. He had apparently been buried beneath the pitch at his own request. There was a look of surprise on his skull because he had meant to add, 'when I die'.

Before starting his fourth hole halfway down the pitch Bunghit stopped and checked that Her Ladyship was still properly knotted. A sixth sense told him that he should have his rifle at hand, and he took it from its binding on the saddle bag and placed it alongside his hostage. Something he had discovered was how much he enjoyed Her Ladyship's company when she was gagged. It was a fact he would bear in mind if he decided to let her live and share the treasure with him.

He was swaying towards letting her survive because he needed somebody with whom to start the next dynasty of Burpas, but the new generation would not grow up as a homeless, wandering tribe of the Khyber Pass. They would have a proper palace roof over their heads, the best education that money could buy (he wondered if it was too late for him to go to Eton to play on their fields), and they would be taught how to use a knife and fork without injuring each other.

Bunghit Din apologised to Her Ladyship for her discomfort. He had not realised that he had covered all of her but her head with a mound of earth from the cricket pitch. 'I will now soon find the treasure, my treasure,' he said. 'And then I will decide what to do with you.'

Her Ladyship replied, 'Mmmm, bstdmmm, ghfgmmmmm smhytmmfcemmm ghmfckmmmm, fghuckmmmmm dfttmmmfck mghcrktmmm...'

It translated as, 'I want to be ungagged and untied. I'm not playing any more of this daft game of cricket.' There may have been one or two unladylike cusses in there that have been left out of this translation to save Lady Ruff-Diamond's blushes.

Bunghit Din returned to his digging, and was beginning to wish that he had been sensible enough to ask his father exactly where under the pitch the treasure had been hidden. It then struck him that as it was nine years since his father had told him the secret on his deathbed perhaps they had used an old pitch alongside the current pitch, as was usually the case at cricket grounds. If necessary he would dig up the entire cricket field. He was determined to find that treasure. It would bankroll the emergence of a bright new generation of Burpas.

The Foot and Mouth search parties were determined to find Her Ladyship. They were scouring every inch of Kalabar, gradually working out to a ten mile radius of Fort Phucka. It was Her Ladyship's bad luck that the cricket field located in the Khasi's palace grounds was right on the perimeter of the search area.

Sergeant-Major Thomas, still in his rugby shirt and shorts, was encouraging his search party with all the enthusiasm and drive of a Welsh scrum leader. 'Come on, boyhos,' he said, 'Only another million nooks and crannies to go. Let's get this ball over the line. Shoulders down, and push. Heel, boyhos, heel.'

'I don't know who's more crackers,' said Arden to McKnacker with his ventriloquist's face. 'Him for the way he talks, or us for listening to him.'

'Och, who's listening tae him,' said McKnacker, who had a musical box stuck to his ear that his grandmother had sold to him on her deathbed. It played the Sugar Plum Fairy from Tchaikovsky's *Nutcracker Suite*. 'I'm concentrating on listening tae the music.'

'But don't you get fed up listening to the same tune over and over again?' said Arden, as he prodded at some straw with his bayonet to make sure Her Ladyship was not hidden under it.

'Och, I deliberately let the musical box wind down so that I hear it at all different speeds,' said McKnacker. 'When I get back hame to bonny Scotland I shall develop the idea. You are looking at the first McKnacker Walkerman.'

Their conversation was disturbed by a sudden shout from a hundred yards away. 'Over here,' came the excited call. 'I've found her... and I've got Bunghit Din as well.'

Arden and McKnacker raced after their torchbearer wallah, and arrived at a tiny smallholding. They had their guns raised, and their fingers on the triggers. In the light thrown out by the flickering flame they made out ordnance officer Bendover. He was pointing his rifle at a couple of pigs.

Sergeant-Major Thomas arrived at the gallop at the same time. 'I grants you that you could make a mistake about Her Ladyship,' admitted the Sergeant-Major. 'But that other one looks nothing like Bunghit Din. Get your heyes seen to, boyho.'

There was another false alarm when Lieutenant

Grimcock, cricket bat swishing, barged his way into a bungalow where he thought he could hear the moans of a terrified woman. He had to beg a thousand, thousand pardons to the grocer Goondha, who was enjoying some spice with one of his store workers. As Lieutenant Grimcock bowed his way out he caught his foot in a mousetrap, and a fox terrier dog snapped at his ankles and made a terrible mess of his cricket whites. 'Next time I come out on one of these infernal searches,' Grimcock said to himself, 'I must remember to wear my pads.'

In the bungalow opposite, Goondhi was doing a roaring trade selling bottles of Piddleade to members of the search parties who were feeling parched in the dry, breathless night air. He had found the way to make his output go farther. He simply put seven eighths water to every eighth of urine. One day, once India had got her long overdue independence, he would follow the advice of the world's worst poet, Mudyard Tipling, and sell franchises. He had even decided on a company name: Pee-Cola.

Back at the Fort, Sir Sidney was in a terrible state. He had wanted to join the search but could not leave the loo.

'I had some of that cold lamb stew when I got here,' he told Captain Ffortescue-Fforetescue. 'I think it has disagreed with me.'

The Great Curry Powder Plot had claimed another victim, and the Governor's only comfort was that Ginga Don, the ever-smiling faithful fanwallah, was on hand to keep him cool with the finest fanning action in the whole of India.

The first light of dawn revealed a range of small hills that had appeared overnight on the Khasi's cricket field. They represented two pitch-worths of earth, and there were two twenty-two-yard long, three-yard wide, eight-foot deep holes. But still no sign of any treasure. Bunghit Din's arms were beginning to get just a little tired, and he was becoming irritated by the snoring rumble coming from Her Ladyship. Even with a gag on, it sounded like the rumble of thunder trapped in a bucket. This had pretty well made up his mind that she would have to be liquidated once he had found the treasure. It was an old Burpa custom that anybody who snored had their throat cut while they slept. Perhaps that was why there were not too many Burpas left, and it also possibly explained why so many of them had been insomniacs. They had simply been too terrified to go to sleep.

Bunghit Din had just finished digging up the second cricket pitch when he realised there was one large area he had not excavated. That was where Her Ladyship was lying. He rolled her over with a prod of his boot, and, quite remarkably, she stopped snoring once she was off her back. Perhaps he would let her share the treasure and the rest of his life after all, provided that she agreed never to sleep on her back.

He had virtually blunted the shovel, but got stuck enthusiastically into the patch where Her Ladyship had been sleeping. Such was his power of motivation that he was mining great mounds of earth with just a couple of digs and shoves, and he had gone down six feet into his latest hole when his shovel struck something solid.

Bunghit Din bent down and cleared the earth surrounding the obstruction with his bare hands. He peered at it, and discovered to his enormous excitement that it was a four-foot square casket with a bevelled lid. Calling on his last ounce of strength, Bunghit Din dragged the casket up and placed it on what little ground was left. He got hold of his rifle and, using the butt, smashed off the padlock and prised open the lid.

Inside was just a slip of paper. It read:

BEAT YOU TO IT - THE MONSTER

The message was just slowly sinking into Bunghit Din's brain when everywhere around him was suddenly a blaze of light as if the sun had fallen down from out of the sky. He looked up from the casket to find the monster galloping towards him with huge flames belching from his mouth.

Half a mile away in the palace, the Khasi had just risen from his bed and was stretching at the window. He saw the sky above the cricket field illuminated by flames, and he wondered why groundsman Ali Grassmowa had not extinguished all the bombfires that had been lit during the previous night's festivities.

Bunghit Din stood the trussed-up Lady Ruff-Diamond on her feet, and held the point of the rifle at her temple. Her Ladyship came out of a deep sleep to see the monster suddenly stop and start pawing at what was left of the ground in front of him. This, she thought, was the most amazing part of the game so far.

'One more flame from you, monster,' said Bunghit

188

Din, 'and Her Ladyship gets it.'

'At last, at last,' she thought.

The Burpas leader dragged his totally confused hostage towards the white charger, and was just about to mount when he felt a vicious crack on the turban. He dropped Her Ladyship to the ground and turned to find a berserk Ali Grassmowa attacking him with a cricket bat.

'Look what you have gone and done to my lovely cricket pitch, you shovelling maniac you,' yelled Ali, pointing at the holes where his pitches used to be. 'I have a match here tomorrow. How in the name of heaven and earth am I going to get it fit for play?'

As Ali raised his bat in anger, Bunghit Din slowly squeezed the trigger on his rifle and fired. In true Burpa traditions, he had forgotten that the gun was pointing at himself. The bullet hit him in the middle of the forehead, and the last of the Burpas dropped slowly backwards into the hole from where he had just lifted the empty treasure casket.

Ali Grassmowa immediately summoned his groundstaff, and they got on with the job of filling in the holes and reparing the pitch for the next day's play.

Her Ladyship fainted into the arms of the monster as he told her in an obviously English-educated voice: 'Don't worry, your Ladyship, I will soon have you back with your husband.'

Her last thought before passing out was, 'Cricket, lousy cricket.'

It was Brother Belcher who returned Her Ladyship to

189

the welcoming arms of her husband, and while they were vowing everlasting love to each other he explained how he had found her left on his mission doorstep by a strange animal that had then run off.

Later, much later, Brother Belcher returned to his mission to count up how much money he had left from selling off the treasure. He had used much of it to finance the Great Curry Powder Plot that had, sadly, been a monumental flop. But there was still enough left, he thought, to help the next Independence Movement that his palms told him would be organised by a man called Gandhi.

Brother Belcher had learned about the whereabouts of the treasure when taking the deathbed confession of Bunghit Din One. He knew that the treasure rightfully belonged to the people of India and not to the Khasi, who had made his fortune by exploiting his fellow Indians and turning them into his slaves. Now Belcher was doing his best to clear his conscience for all the plundering that the British had done in the name of Her Majesty Queen Victoria, God bless her. He would keep quietly encouraging them towards Independence, and he would, whenever necessary, continue to bring out his monster costume and the flame-throwing tricks he had learned from his father in London's markets.

When the Governor and his reunited wife returned hand-in-hand to their house of residence, Sir Sidney ordered the chefwallah to prepare lunch – 'anything but bloody lamb stew,' he said.

'I will heat up the lightly curried chicken that I was

preparing for yesterday's meal,' said the chefwallah.

It was some eight hours later that Sir Sidney and Lady Ruff-Diamond sat in adjoining toilets feeling as if their behinds were being blown off.

'What a bloody carry on,' said Sir Sidney as the ever-smiling, ever-faithful Ginga Don fanned him.

'Yes, I agree,' Her Ladyship said from the other side of the wall. 'It's been quite a curry on up the Khyber.'

WHATEVER HAPPENED TO...

Sir Sidney and Lady Ruff-Diamond were given a new posting to Australia where they uncovered a plot to make the country a Republic. Sir Sidney tried to drink Australia dry and Her Ladyship disappeared with a man in an iron mask calling himself Ned Kelly Two.

Goondhi became a piddle peddler, bottling his secret recipe and becoming a ruPEE billionaire.

Ginga Don became a bicycle pedaller, and set up the biggest taxi service in Kalabar... employing the **Khasi** when his shopping-until-they-were-dropping wives made him bankrupt.

Brother Belcher failed to predict the Wall Street Crash and lost all the treasure money that he had invested.

Mudyard Tipling returned home to England where he was made Poet Laureate.

Captain Ffortescue-Ffortescue, Sergeant-Major Thomas and **Lieutenant Grimcock** all went 'over the top' in the First World War. When will they ever learn? When will they ever learn?

191

DON'T MISS THE OTHER HILARIOUS TITLES IN THIS **CARRY ON** SERIES

And don't forget that all the *Carry On* classics are also available on the Cinema Club video label, and distributed by VCI, price £4.99 each. Watch the videos, read the books... and *Carry On laughing.*